GA

GREENWOOD & ARCHER
PUBLISHING LLC

Shaina Thomas
07.15.18

Sophia, Thank you
So much for your
constant
support
You are
amazing !!!!!

SHAINA THOMAS

Tulsa's Legacy

A NOVEL

Greenwood & Archer Publishing LLC
Tulsa, OK

DEDICATION

"I don't know what you're going to be, but you're going to be something," these words were spoken by my Grandfather who purchased a laptop for me after hitting big at the casino. During my early years in high school, he had taken note of the hours I would spend walking to the library, reading and writing. This debut novel is dedicated to those like him who planted seeds in my heart, especially while witnessing a granddaughter navigating the world without her mother. Special dedication to my siblings who cried, laughed and conquered. To Craig who tuned in on the other end of the phone as I read for hours, hours at a time reading chapter after chapter of my early writing projects. You enthusiastically asked questions and tracked every characters' move!

Special gratitude and love extended to Ethel Ross Waugh, my God Mother, who I first met as an academic counselor at McLain High School (later renamed, McLain High School for Science and Technology) in Tulsa, Oklahoma. You invited me into your home and informed me about the Gates Millennium Scholarship that granted me access to higher education.

Thank you for declaring that I had a gift of speaking and writing.

CONTENTS

Prologue

PART ONE: Spring's Kiss

PART TWO: Summer's Debt

Acknowledgments

To the Writers, Historians, Sociologists and Researchers who have preserved such history. To All Readers, in hopes that this novel serves as an additional piece that illuminates the lives and generations of those tied to such a vibrant part of American and global history. Here are a very few of the many people who made this book possible:

My once living reflection of God, Paula Annette Middleton, my late Mother who convinced me that a stick-figured drawing in my early years was a brilliant sketch. She even asked could I teach her how to draw that same pitiful picture. In that moment, she taught me the power of love and praise. She introduced me to a talent that would later aid in financial support as I attended a four-year university. Donald "Red Bird" Middleton, my dancing, drinking and gambling Grandfather who was full of so much life and who bought me my first laptop after winning big at the local casino and replaced it after it was stolen from an uncle when I began writing an early novel. To my siblings, Jeron, Sonya, Craig Middleton and Nia Linzy who inspired my first writing installment that sits in old flash-drives waiting on my attention. Special thanks to Craig who kept me lifted while I was away in college. Sonya, who was always eager to read my novel and to support me in everything that I do. Ethel Waugh, my God Mother who also welcomed me into her home church – the historic Vernon A.M.E. Chapel – located in Tulsa's Greenwood District. Thank you for declaring my talents as gifts. Extended family members and friends who have read excerpts after excerpts of any novel that I started and did not quite complete from 2009 to the present. To everyone and every experience that spoke life into my visions and who genuinely smiled back when I shared them: Lynn and Ms. Jefferson, Jet, 'Maine, Onrea and extended family. Lisa. Aimee. Trent. Dr. Hill. Lupe Davidson. Colleagues. Italya. Christa. Nielah. Shay. Pastor Michelle K.T. Moulden and Vernon Family. Cordarrow Milton who served as inspiration through your own persistence and dedication to your works. Grandma Miranda who reminded me of Purpose. To Kerry Linzy who referred to me as "Super Star" whenever I used to get so hard on myself. Most importantly, to the generations, victims and survivors of the Tulsa Race Riot/Massacre of 1921.

When my right foot hit the ground, I heard it. I felt it. At the same time. My lower back. The worst pain I had ever known. Not like scraping a knee, but indescribable. Pain that cannot be fixed. I wanted to reach for it and cover it, but my hands caught the ground. More pain. In my knee, the left one. The dirt smelt like summer. Like the Fourth of July, but it wasn't Independence Day. Was it? What day is it? It had to be July. The pain. July. The heat. June? The choking. May? Yes, May. It didn't feel like May. The parade. I remember. Memorial Day. May.

May? No, June.

"The railroad tracks! Go to the tracks!" It was a distant warning.

My body was heavy and my feet were bare. My legs ran beneath me, but I wasn't going anywhere. The ground was warm. There was shooting. Somewhere close. Shouting. My legs kept running. I couldn't feel my heart, but I was breathing. Yes, I was still breathing. The black smoke rising from the ground tasted bitter in my throat and burned. I was choking, but I had to keep going. If I had not heard the gunshots and the screaming, I would have stopped to catch my breath. To feel my heart. To look, one last time.

As quickly as possible, I glanced over my right shoulder. I could not recognize them, but there were people there. Small crowds fled past the shadows. Illuminated by the light. Fires. I was far behind. Too far. Closer to the gunshots. Maybe too close, but I could make it. Had to make it. If I went faster, it was possible. When my right foot hit the ground, I heard it. I felt it. At the same time. My lower back. The worst pain I had ever known.

SPRING, S KISS

Chapter One
On Purpose

I broke the sixth commandment when I was twelve years old.

It felt nothing like the guilt when swatting at flies, spiders and bugs. It was a quick decision. One I had to make. I think.

My brother, Nelson, had just turned twenty-three. A.C. Freeman, the porter, was back from up North. The tourist showed up around the same time that he did.

The tourist. That is what I called her before I ever knew her name. She saw it all happen. Coming into town before the summer's war.

"We were an accident waiting to happen, A.C. and I."

That's how she began to explain it.

Only, I did not agree.

I watched her ease the oversized fedora from her head. A gift from her father who died in the Great War. Her hair was full. Curly. Wild. Free. Like her. Her eyes danced across the sky, stopped. Lingered. A smile swept over her full lips. Her face, a canvas for a light touch of makeup, and yet; she wore none. Gazed over at me. Her eyes examined mine, but she was not present. She was there. I remembered.

So did she.

February 6, 1921 | Sunday

"Wait here."

I waited. Watched. Like I always did.

I tracked the sound of laughter to my left. The Carlton family was returning from their weekend trip to Georgia. I returned the wide wave to their youngest son while the eldest dropped his smile and looked away like he was bothered to see me. We had bad history after he tried to spread lies about my family. Well, John-Jon, was not exactly blood family; but he and his folks have been around mine so long that he felt like kin.

I watched the Carlton family go on about their way. Like most days, Sundays welcomed families into busy parlors for shopping.

Familiar faces, waving hands and loud conversations. Reminders to be polite to kids too young to care. Weather did not matter much. Cold winds, perfect warmth or sticky heat; there was always people talking and going somewhere. All ages. With a purpose. Buying this, eating that. Playing this and watching that. In grocers, two theatres, pool halls and restaurants. Getting or providing services here and there at doctors' or realtors' offices. Rooming houses and hotels. Passing each other in and out of red brick buildings lining either side of a dusty trail near the railroad tracks. A lot of folks traveled from Archer, the street of the Depot, and then swarmed Deep Greenwood like flies ready for summer. From the intersection of Greenwood Avenue and Archer Street, Deep Greenwood stretched to the north. It flooded into our world of what felt like a city-within-a-city long before I knew anything about it.

That was as far as I was able to see.

Pine Street to the North. Cincinnati Street on the West. Lansing Street on the East. Standpipe Hill where doctors, lawyers and owners of the businesses lived near Independence Street. Residences sprouted throughout. Finally, Greenwood to Archer. For me, our world—the Negro District—was like the most luxurious cruise ship in the world. White Tulsa surrounded us like looming ocean currents. Not being permitted to cross the tracks made me curious about all of Tulsa. It was the law. Well, unless I leave school for a job in white Tulsa working for a white family somewhere on the other side of the tracks. Then, I would be able to see everything. All I can imagine were the things I have heard or what I read. Or assumed. Or what my Pa would talk about with folks.

My Pa owned one of the best department stores on Greenwood. I call it the Glass House because it is so nice. Red brick three-story building with an entrance covered in windows. Strolling by the outside of it, folks could see people walking around inside checking out Pa's handiwork. They were usually accompanied by Pa who kept them talking and shopping. His hands would move about as his bright smile stole the show between conversations. Once they made their selections, he would escort them to the glass counter with a fancy machine on it. A colossal chandelier hung from the ceiling and was visible to the left when standing in front of the counter. By the time I was old enough to walk, Pa would let me tag along to spend the day with him at the store. For years, Momma and Pa, did not have a motorcar. Does not matter much, having one or not, because we walk everywhere most of the time anyhow. When I was old enough to make the walk alone, I began to see the porter. A.C. Freeman, the preacher's son.

I saw him a lot, back then. Before he left. Whenever I would see him walking, I remember catching up with him. "Where are you going," I would wait on his answer. Look up at him. I followed whatever his answer was with asking, "Why?" His replies were trailed with another question from me. I pried, because I wished I was as free as him. He went wherever he wanted to go no matter who had anything to say about it. Especially church folk. He did not care too much for being the subject of gossip. Did not matter if his father was the head of our church. Back then, with all my questioning, I was too young to know getting in his business was impolite.

I made the mistake of telling Pa and Momma the things A.C. had shared with me about Jazz halls. Of course, he had told me all of what he did because I had asked about them all the time.

"Who do you see in there," I asked once.

He smirked, a little. Looked ahead. "It would be quite the surprise to you." When he said – you – his voice went up like he knew something I did not know. *You.* Like someone I knew had gone to those Jazz halls. His response made me curious. Weighed the odds.

I asked Pa if he had ever gone. In return, thanks to Momma, I found out that there was a limit to how many questions I could ask someone. That it was not my place to ask adults about their whereabouts. After that, I did not ask A.C. many questions anymore. Except, the last time I spoke with A.C., he was talking to me about the world real funny-like. Like there was something I was missing out on. Like Greenwood and places like it had more to offer for folks older than me.

I wonder what he has seen. What he has experienced, since then. Sitting in an empty wagon near the Frisco Depot on Archer Street, I spotted him. There I was minding everybody else's business and he came out of the Depot wearing what looked like a porter's uniform. Navy blue, white collar tucked behind a navy jacket with gold round buttons. No porter's cap, but a fedora. A weird mix. It was a wonder to me that he had returned. For good? There was gossip from the elders about A.C. He was known not to keep quiet whenever it was appropriate. Some say he was thrown in jail after the trouble in Chicago two years ago. They say he went in talking. Police could not shut him up so they just beat him. When I spotted him near the Depot, I tried to see any signs of ever being in the riot. He did not look beaten. For a riot that lasted from the end of July to the start of August, he sure did not have any signs of having been hurt. Maybe there has been enough time for healing. Back then, folks seemed to be fighting everywhere except here. The trouble in Chicago had to be the deadliest fight in the country that I had ever read about in Tulsa newspapers here in Greenwood. They say there was blood in the streets. A.C. was there and arrested, for something. I wanted to find out if it were really for his mouth.

I figure, in America, trouble was just the kind of thing to expect when white folks get angry with us. Though, I really have not seen too many whites long enough to know anything about their temperament. All of what I got was what I read in the 'papers like the lynching, sharecropping and keeping us out of parts of town and some schools. They liked us apart. Neighborhoods, churches, schools and universities. We had Howard University way off on the east of the United States. I read about Howard all the time in the Tulsa Star. The Tulsa Star newspaper was owned by Andrew Jackson Smitherman; a fancy Negro man I think was by way of Muskogee, Oklahoma who had a sense of humor you had to think about twice. In the 'paper, I always read the section that congratulates the graduating classes. All Negros. I hope no trouble does anything to Howard before I am old enough to go. There always seemed to be trouble in places far away. I wanted Tulsa to remember me and I wanted my name right there in Tulsa Star as a graduate from the Howard University. Doing what, I don't know. I just wanted to do whatever would let me be an adult, spy and tell stories.

I guess I would not make for much of a spy and storyteller if I did not get down to the reasons for this and that. Down to the facts. I knew a lot about them, but I had no idea why the trouble and fighting like in Chicago would happen or what A.C. was doing back in town. I promised myself I would figure it all out by the end of the summer.

He walked from the Depot tipping his hat to those who said their *howdies* and hellos. He never seemed to notice me. Or the crowds. He just kept on walking. Walking toward Greenwood with a trunk in his left hand. After all the years of being away, I cannot imagine that was all he possessed. I wanted to follow him, but remembered Momma would be back soon. I stayed put. Waited. Watched. And then I saw her. The tourist. She was a short woman, but somehow stood tall. Serious eyes. Dark eyebrows. No makeup. No earrings. No lipstick. Her hair was covered by a fedora a few sizes too big. No dress. Brown trousers, loose. Stitched by a mother for travel, I imagined. White blouse. Dusty boots on her feet. Pigskin luggage falling from both hands. Like my grandmother's. She stumbled from the exit of the train car, melting into the pulse of the crowd. Her mouth parted, but nothing came out. She looked around. Smiled. There was a commotion across Archer Street in front of the Depot that made her mouth turn up with her chin. She searched. Jess' Semple[1], an elder known for his outbursts, was shouting his disapproval. There was a note attached to a pole. Jess' went for it. Later, I would read it: NOTICE TO IWW'S: DON'T LET THE SUN SET ON YOU IN TULSA. —VIGILANCE COMMITTEE. Whatever that meant. She watched. I watched. There was uncertainty in her eyes. She didn't know where to go. Lawrence Freeman, Pastor Freeman's eldest son who was much taller and broader than his younger brother, approached her from the left. His mouth moved. From my spot sitting atop a wagon, I could not hear. I wondered if he knew her. Close by, Jess' was being escorted through the people by his wife. He followed her small frame, howling, *"We built this here country with our labor!"* He shouted over the hum of preoccupied voices. Folks moved fast. Talking. Living. No one seemed to be listening, but we heard him. Like always. A family passed by and claimed a nearby wagon that was not holding a twelve-year-old. I searched the crowd again. They were still there. Mr. Lawrence's mouth moved and this time, she responded. I needed to learn how to read lips. I narrowed my eyes. It did not help. She lowered a suitcase, offered a hand. Mr. Lawrence took it. His attention shifted. I followed their gaze. He waved at someone. At Mr. Stradford,

---

[1] Langston Hughes, *The Best of Simple Stories* (New York: Hill & Wang, 1961).

who owned the great Negro hotel in the Nation. According to the 'papers. I shifted my attention just a little more to the right. To him.

A.C. walked boldly toward them. He stood taller; more like Pa and not like my big-headed brother Nelson. Balanced shoulders. His hat lowered to his chest in courtesy. His free hand extended out to her.

"Let's go." Momma. Standing to my left. Wearing one of her large hats and beautiful white dresses. "How about you come down from there. Mrs. Janette will be here soon. Let's wait on her in the taxi. One more stop and then back home."

Home.

Chapter Two
Home

". . . A Negro empire built upon the ruins of southern homes and institutions" . . . "Supremacy of the white race in social, political and governmental affairs of the nation."[2]

It was words on the front page of Tulsa's Tribune newspaper. A newspaper a couple days old that I noticed in the sitting room the night before. It was words that brought laughter out of Pa's gut after he read them. He tossed the 'papers and pointed a finger at me. I stopped near the door. Waited.

"You oughta be proud," he was grinning.

I grinned back, helplessly. "For what, Pa,"

"Proud of where you are! Proud that we don't have to read this trash and have our own 'papers," he smiled with every word. "I bet the owner of their 'papers be out there waving his torch. See'em all the time up on Standpipe Hill. Like that ol' silly picture *Birth of a Nation* that folks cannot get enough of 'round here," sound like he was talking more to himself than to me.

"Why do they say the things they say about where we live," I slipped my hand from the doorknob. My friends could wait.

"Don't let me stop you. Go on out, we'll talk more about it another time."

We did not always live on Elgin. Sometime before I was ever born, my family moved into town from another state. Another city. We, the Lavelles and Martins, came to Tulsa and populated Elgin Street a bit further down the way away from Deep Greenwood. Well, just my brother Nelson and our Momma and Pa lived on Elgin. Momma's parents stayed

---

[2] Tim Madigan, *The Burning: Massacre, Destruction, and the Tulsa Race Riot of 1921* (New York: St. Martin's Press, 2001): 32.

7

closer to Greenwood on Detroit. Gran'ma Jordan and Gran'pa Skip. Though, Gran'pa Skip died in a small town somewhere riding back in to the state of Oklahoma from Texas a year after I was born. They say he never made it out of a small town near Houston. Momma's side, the Martins, were in Texas all over. Some in California and places in between. Most of the Lavelles stayed in Louisiana, Georgia or wandered in during the holidays from places I had never heard of. Mostly places in the south region of the United States. Though, our people did not like the south much and moved quite a bit to get away from it.

Pa has an older sister somewhere in France I have never met. He said she left because she could never stomach American politics as a Negro woman and disappeared as soon as she could. I always wondered what was so great about France that she had to move there. Why not one of the countries in Africa? I heard a lot about moving back to Africa these days. After the war ended. A race man named Garvey, who had gotten shot somewhere for starting trouble, was known for talking about going back to Africa. Back, like most of us Negros in America had been there in this day and age. I read it in the 'papers Pa would leave lying around the house. The 'papers made Garvey sound like he was not afraid to share how he felt concerning how things were for Negros in America. It mentioned a place called Liberia. I wondered, if Liberia – how Garvey imagined it to be – felt anything like Greenwood. Or, if France could compare to how my aunt was experiencing it. Wondered if she had stayed would she be satisfied with the Tulsa we knew. Wondered if Garvey would be pleased if he knew what Negro folks were doing in Tulsa, right *here* in America. Wondered if either of them knew what I knew. What Pa, A.C. Freeman and everybody else seemed to know.

I walked outside not minding the cold too much on my way to school. A dusty road, two blocks over and past the crazy Dillard family who had a lot of kids they had to help get ready for school. Hector, the last middle child, came running down the steps in his trousers, hat, bare feet and no shirt like clockwork. I ran after him, scooping him up in my arms. He was getting heavier these days. Spoiled, my Gran'ma Jordan would say. Get and eat whatever it was that he begged and cried for. He laughed wild and asked me what I was planning to do. He reminded me of myself, so I planted him on his feet and gave him something to think about.

"What do you see when you look around?"

He searched. His body wobbled left and right. Belly sitting out from the rest of him, satisfied. It was not like the south, but all of Tulsa was like the south. Tulsa was the south, but considered Midwest because it was in Oklahoma. It felt like it. I mean, people were separated like it. So, for me, it was the south. Though, most of the time, where we live made you forget about all of that.

"Home!" His thin arm stretched a tiny hand to point a finger at his house. His laughter wild again when Mrs. Dillard came running out the door thanking me for catching him. She popped him on his bottom and pulled him up the stairs by the arm. I held back my smile when he looked over his shoulder to see if I was still watching.

I walked off, smiling. Feeling good. Proud. The best thing that ever happened to me was that I was born in Tulsa, Tulsa's Greenwood. An elder told me once that Greenwood was named for a city in Mississippi. I have never been to Mississippi, but I cannot think of any other place like Tulsa's Greenwood. Booker T. Washington himself called it the Negro Wall Street. Home. It was home to me. No matter how many people kept on coming and no matter how many parlors opened for business, it was home. Folks say that it was a land that had been ignored by white folks who thought it was useless. Then, we came. We came, built, owned and sold our land after Tulsa struck gold – well, oil. Other folks say there were Negros and Natives here long before Oklahoma even became a state. We talk about it in school. Everybody says that Greenwood was all possible because of Negro men and women like Gurley and Stradford who owned the most

9

amazing properties in Tulsa. The Stradford Hotel was one of the largest hotels I had ever seen. Not that I had seen or stayed in many across the world, but it sure looked better than the hotels in the 'papers. Larger, fuller. Folks in Greenwood were proud people like Stradford and Gurley. It is no wonder people kept on coming.

New folks in town did not have to do much but step foot out of the Depot and choose a hotel or room for rent with all the hotels and renting rooms around. From Archer Street to the intersection where folks ran right into Deep Greenwood and on down the way. Beautiful hotels. The places to stay, that people usually knew about first, was the Stradford Hotel at 301 on Greenwood and O.W. Gurley's hotel. They are the richest men I knew. Folks say they were here and rich long before I was ever born. Long before they had ever come to Tulsa. Their properties did not stand alone. Huff's hotel. Phillips. Titus. Morgan. Carr. Sanders. Mr. Warren's three-story hotel, IMPERIAL and Hotel Small that really was not that small for a three-story building itself. Strassner hotel was down on Cameron Street, three-story. Thinking about all the hotels, I wondered where the tourist from the depot was staying. Wondered what happened after seeing her meet with A.C. and Lawrence Freeman. Thought about her oversized fedora, the trousers and the boots.

The shopping was not too bad for newcomers or visitors.

There were clothing, shoe, hats and dress shops. You had to be here a little longer to know that there was a variety of dresses on Second Street in downtown Tulsa at the Cohn's, a Jewish store some blocks from Greenwood in white Tulsa. If I had any control over it, I would not have known much about no dresses, but when you have a mother like mine, there was no way around it. She loved new dresses for as many church services as possible.

There were benefits that came with her as my mother. She was always busy. Always speaking. Usually at churches or meetings where kids could not go. I figured it was about politics, but that wasn't too much fun to listen in on anyhow. If she wasn't speaking, she was always willing to help folks on Greenwood or folks' happenings at churches. She was the first person I followed around to learn much of what I knew.

In following her around Tulsa, I discovered that one of the perfect places to hide and watch visitors, newcomers and natives were at the intersection of Archer and Greenwood where all the moving happened. You could see who was coming and who was going. Deep Greenwood had more to tell near the intersection by Archer. The heart. It woke up with the sun, but danced with the moon. With cooler and warmer weather, it knocked on doors and brought more families, friends, acquaintances and enemies to the parlors for longer periods at a time. It breathed the smell of food, coffee, perfumes and life. It provided a sanctuary for the righteous and sinners. Preachers and prostitutes. Smaller children and elders. Deep Greenwood was the fullest area on Greenwood with Colored folks' businesses everywhere lining both sides of the unpaved road. The Glass House was deep in Greenwood, too. They say that's where the first business, a grocer shop, was built. Then a Negro real estate developer, a dentist, physician and Baptist minister grew the community along Archer Street that ran parallel to the Frisco railroad track. Where I would hide on occasions.

Hiding was necessary when I wanted to find out things elders did not want me to know. Silent questions that I was not allowed to ask was likely to be answered when being quiet and just watching folks. If I was lucky, I could hide near or inside of an empty wagon to eavesdrop on the people coming and going. Plenty of people would notice me, but they would forget about me and go on about their business so long as I kept my mouth shut. Every morning, when I woke up with the sun on days with no school, I was ready to run out to Deep Greenwood.

I remember when I was about Hector's age, walking to the Glass House. The time I had ran into A.C. before he took off to Chicago. He noticed me lingering behind, avoiding him. He asked why I was not asking any questions all of a sudden. I shared with him what Pa and Momma told me about being polite. He smiled a little and told me to never stop asking questions. Then, he asked me a question that I was not too sure how to answer.

"What do you see when you look around?"

I looked. Trees. Dirt. Sun. No more clouds. "Um, I don'know," I didn't know what to say then. Hector's answer would have been perfect.

His head lowered and his arm wrapped around my shoulder. His right hand sliced the air for a second time. "Look again," his voice was a whisper near my ear.

We took a few steps forward while I looked, squinting. There were the brick buildings of businesses and the Rowlands' block of little shotgun rent houses to the north near larger ones built by the Mann brothers. The road, the trees, grass, the sun and us. It was getting hot. "Um," I did not know what else to say.

His head sprung upward, "Ownership," his arm fell from my shoulder and I watched his eyes dance. I followed his steps. "You may not understand this now, but when someone rents a room they are paying someone else to stay there. There is nothing wrong with renting as you are making plans to build and own. But, if you own your home, that money is an investment. That investment multiplies. It is an investment in stability. Stability to properly raise a family and build a community. A strong community."

"Investment? Stability?"

He lowered; his mouth was next to my right ear as he pointed to G. E. Floor & Roofing Co. "A house cannot be built without a foundation. Without a foundation, the house will collapse. For example, that store, owned by G. E.—,"

"G. E. Wilson," I finished. Greenwood was growing, but everyone was familiar. He nodded. "To build that foundation, you need supplies. There is a need. Call that a demand. G. E. can provide the service. Call that supply. Supply and demand. The money that is used for G. E.'s services circulates through this community," he points to a Café. "Let's say Wilson drinks coffee and spends his money there," he points to a cleaners, "And takes his suits there,"

"The money circulates," I make a circle with an index finger. His armpit was warm on my shoulder.

"Yes, the money *circulates*—imagine, about thirty-six times—and Greenwood remains economically independent. Stability. Self-sufficient. Foundation. Strong. To maintain that stability," he points at the Washington's, a small family of three, walking by Pa's department store. "Let's say John's mother works at the Café and his father works at G. E.

12

Floor & Roofing Co. and both save their money at the bank," he glances at me. "They save enough to build or buy a house. Or get supplies or furniture from your Father's department store. They become owners of a home to raise a family and that boy grows up to possibly take over a family business—his mother's Café," his eyes looked over his shoulder. I followed his gaze toward the homes.

The porches didn't look as depressed as I had remembered. When compared to the massive mansions, owned by White folks across Main Street, it had been easy to convince myself that Negroes did not have much.

"Who owns Greenwood," I asked.

I understood it now. His smile was full of pride. Pride that Pa talked about. His back straightened and his hand gripped my shoulder firmly. "We do. And if there were no businesses in Greenwood, there will be no jobs in our community,"

"The homes?"

"Would be built by someone else and probably only for us to rent," he was certain.

"Someone else," I repeated, but I knew the answer.

"*Someone else*," he looked forward. His eyes gazed around. "What do you see now?"

"Segregation," I had heard the word before.

His head spun and his eyes searched mine. I could not read his expression, but he did not appear surprised. He looked more like he was choosing his words carefully. "In some cases, segregation is necessary for the healing process," his voice was faint like he was thinking aloud. "When you are living in a society that historically and currently abuses your people in a number of ways, there must be some separation to recover. This," his eyes danced, "Is recovery."

"*Politics*," I complained.

He laughed, nodded. "Economics,"

"I don't understand,"

"Give it some time," he straightened his back, tipped his hat and grinned. With a smirk, he sung *Little Africa* in a tune like church folk.

That was the last time I saw him before he left. I started thinking

13

about Greenwood differently after speaking with him. For Greenwood, over the years since he left, A.C. was like the thoughts in the back of a person's mind. He returned rarely, but when he did; there was a great cause for it. He was always known as a race man. As trouble, to elders who saw fit for him to stay in his place and to just keep quiet. Though, he was not just a talker like Jess' Semple, who also served his purpose in Greenwood. Never being afraid to speak his mind. A.C. was about action and talk later. There was no need in looking for trouble, folks say. I guess he went looking and Chicago did something to him. He came back quietly this time. Calm.

I saw the calm daze in his eyes. In his posture. In his walk. I saw it when he greeted her. I thought about it a little more, all day. About the stories in the 'papers. With him back, nothing felt the same. To make things stranger, something unusual happened after school.

Normally, I would fall into the habit of walking home as the third to what made my closest friends and me the Trio. This time, there was a motorcar waiting for me. Momma stood in front of the closed door. Taxi driver looking my way. There was a veil over her face. Gloves on her hands. Full, dark dress. Heels.

"Your Father is out of town with Nelson. I have a meeting to attend at First Baptist. You will be joining me."

Chapter Three
Little Africa

"Niggertown" or "Little Africa"
Jones, Tulsa's Tribune Newspaper Owner

"A bad nigger is about the lowest thing that walks on two feet. Give a bad nigger his booze and his dope and a gun and he thinks he can shoot up the world. And all these four things are to be found in Niggertown, booze, dope, bad niggers and guns.[3]"

Across the tracks.

We saw them and they saw us.

They stood there like mad dogs. It was five of them, three of us. The Trio. They were all sizes, but my eyes stayed on the one with the double chin and mean eyes. His eyes. Blue, like the ocean, but missing the reflection of God. I made sure not to budge. Not to stay in my place. Closer to the tracks than I was supposed to be. Closer to them. So close, I could smell them. One of them smelt like my memories or New Orleans's swamps.

"Look at those niggers," it was a girl standing to Blue Eye's right. She was very thin. Her voice much thinner. Squeaky. Her white dress was perfect. Her dark hair was pulled low in a braided pigtail and covered at the top with a small hat. Blue Eye's shirt and trousers were smeared with dried mud. His four disciples were clean.

"They cain't speak," she laughed. It sounded more like choking.

"*Can't*," John-Jon corrected. Sometimes, when we were in the comfort of our own company, we spoke improperly. Like with elders, this moment was different.

"Wha'chu say, *boy*?" Blue Eyes stepped forward. Ellen and I stepped back. John-Jon stayed where he was.

John-Jon wasn't the toughest guy in Tulsa, but looking at him then,

---

[3] Tim Madigan, *The Burning: Massacre, Destruction, and the Tulsa Race Riot of 1921* (New York: St. Martin's Griffin, 2001): 215-216.

no one would have ever known he was a little funny. Funny, meaning he did not seem comfortable playing with the boys so he made it a habit to tag along with Ellen and I. Like always, in that very moment, I was thankful he was there. "Don't worry about him," Pigtail grabbed Blue Eye's arm. "Go back to Little Africa," her brown eyes scanned ours. They lingered on John-Jon's. For just a split second, I believe guilt washed over her face. "Come on boys and girls," she tugged at her messiah's arm. "Let's find something better to do."

The walk from the tracks was quiet. Ellen was the first to speak.

"I'm not from Africa," her voice was low. Her face twisted like she was in deep pain. "Do I look like I'm from Africa?" Her arms waved in the air like she was pleading with God.

"You're black," John-Jon kicked a rock of dirt. It barely made it into the air before shattering into dust.

Made in His image. I silently thought about the image of God.

"I'm brown," her chin rose, arms lowered to her sides. Her eyes watched John-Jon.

"You're still a nigger,"

She punched his shoulder. We stopped. I watched them.

He apologized. "What's wrong with being from Africa," he challenged her.

"I am not a slave," she tossed back.

"You have to be a slave to be from Africa?"

She shrugged. He exhaled, shook his head. We stood there. Her eyes grew distant. Ellen was beautiful. She had hair that could be pulled back like Pigtail's. Long, straight. Her skin was not as light as she thought it was, but she was not as dark as me. Momma always told me that all skin was beautiful, so I did not think I was less beautiful because Ellen was lighter. But, I think Ellen believes I am. She had a habit of comparing us; often times concluding that she looked better in clothes and hats than I did. Whenever her Pa could afford to buy her new things. I have learned to ignore it. John-Jon had smooth dark skin, darker than the both of ours. He never seemed ashamed.

"Let's go home," Ellen finally pressed.

"Little Africa it is," I led the troops.

Chapter Four
Jazz & Religion

I was leaving.

I knew it before they told me.

The summer kicked back and let spring showers linger. Pregnant raindrops tap-danced across the house's windows. Like music. Like my parents. The smell of my mother's ham and Pa's bacon filled our small shotgun house. The music against my bedroom window and the smells of breakfast made my body jerk forward. I jumped up and out of bed, spun in the middle of the room and hit my knee on the crooked wooden table Pa made last Christmas. A table he did not want to sell, but one Momma liked because she said it had *personality*. Which, was sort of funny to me, because it ended up tucked away in my room. My throat nearly cursed it before I could suppress it. I swore in groans loud enough to be heard.

"Get in here and eat and don't forget to say grace!"

A familiar warning.

Momma is one of those southern mothers who believed in going to church every day of the week. There was no way around it, believe me, I have tried. Toothache? Go to church, *God will fix it*. Jammed ankle? Second pew. Chickenpox? Back pew and do not touch the other kids. Have a sore throat – conveniently – on youth Sunday? No, you may not skip out on choir. Vernon was an A.M.E. African Methodist Episcopal church. I could never get that right. The last word always came out like I couldn't control my tongue. *Epsikabable*. I hated whenever I had to say it all out the way Pastor Freeman does. Whenever I came across some kid who did not know what denomination African Methodist *Epsikabable* was, I would just shrug and say it was like all churches just with a different name. Different name, same God. At least that's how Momma explained it once. Gran'ma Jordan never quite agreed with that though, but she did not agree with much. She was unforgiving and not much like God at all. To me.

I remember the first time I invited Ellen to Vernon. Her family did

17

not go to church much back then, which isn't normal for any family around here. I guess the heavens opened up like the elders' saying goes and Ellen just up and decided to convince her folks to come. When they did, I formally introduced Ellen to my grandmother. Though, Gran'ma Jordan already knew about her and her family. Gran'ma Jordan was a proud elder who was tall and thin, but in great health. She had full cheekbones that set high. She always had this look where her eyes gazed down the bridge of her nose. Her lips would not move much when she spoke. Her posture had been perfected over the years of forcing us to learn proper etiquette in church pews. Her hair was always straightened and pinned under a cloth hat that rich folks were starting to wear. No strand of hair fell in the wrong places.

"You would be such a pretty young lady, if you wore clothes that fit," Gran'ma Jordan's jawline was stiff. She was gazing downward. Like usual.

Ellen smiled back and simply said, "Well, Ms. Martin, I ain't got many Sunday clothes, but God wouldn't mind that, *would He*?" Ellen was smart like that. That's why I hung out with her. We hung on each other's arm everywhere we went until some elder would see us coming and reminded us how old we were and that it was beginning to become inappropriate. They didn't know Ellen was like a sister to me. Closer to me than the brother Momma and Pa decided to have ten years prior to having me.

Nelson was mean. Not mean to me, but to people. Not that I am not a person, but other people. *People, people*. Mean to women to be concrete, but that is another story. A story Gran'ma Jordan would not exactly consider *proper* to talk about. Family issues were family issues and not to be shared outside of the home. There's nothing more to say about that. Well, the day when Gran'ma Jordan met Ellen – had she known any better – she would have appreciated Ellen for responding the way that she did. Ellen did not tell Gran'ma Jordan the business going on in her home. Did not tell her the news that her Pa lost his job in white Tulsa and that her Momma's pay from cleaning in one of those mansions on the Southside across the tracks was not enough to attend to new clothes. I thought that was funny. The fact that Gran'ma Jordan was always

18

commenting on other folks' lives while hiding her own. The fact that Ellen's mother worked in a mansion, but still did not have much money was funny too. Some white folks were weird like that. Or, maybe it's just the world. What did the Bostons, the wealthy family Ellen's mother worked for, have to lose? While Ellen was short on Sunday clothes, seemed like the Bostons had everything. Ellen told me about the Model T that shined like a new penny, the closets full of clothes, the chandeliers and the big furniture and beautiful kitchen. Probably had more than Gran'ma Jordan's old bungalow.

Anyway, Momma wasn't like that. Like Gran'ma Jordan, I mean. Momma was kind, but firm. When she got fired up about something, the whole family knew about it and if she had anything to say about it, we were equally passionate. Though, I was usually more passionate about Momma's grits, eggs, ham and toast that decorated the table most mornings. Sometimes, Pa would make his bacon with some secret seasoning that made it taste a little sweet. It was a perfect combination to balance out the saltiness. I did not waste any time plopping down across from Pa, ignoring the numb pain in my knee.

The normal routine was breakfast in our crowded kitchen in the back of the house at our bulky table that was too nice for such a small space. Everyone would be dressed in their Sunday's best. Pa would sing some tune under his breath from the Jazz clubs. Momma would cut her eye in his direction and he would smile. Wink. She would hold back a grin. Jazz and religion did not mix. At least not for some folks. To me, that was Momma and Pa. He was like Jazz: forbidden. Gran'ma Jordan did not like his side of the family much so that made her weary of him. He always had this fresh air and newness about him that brought a permanent bounce to his walk. His smile always set on the left corner of his face. His eyes moved like they held a joke no one else was in on. He had his own beat. His own tune. He was Pa. Momma? Momma is traditional. She was like the cross on the wall near the kitchen table. Sacred, holding on to so much meaning beyond herself. Every holiday, every birthday, and every day of the week Momma kept things in order. I guess that's one thing she had in common with Gran'ma Jordan. Only, Momma had a soft spot for Jazz. For the forbidden fruit. Pa and Momma. They were the perfect sin, if at all.

Pa was not singing that morning. Momma did not start the prayer before eating, but this did not excuse the prayer. It only meant that we had to do it ourselves instead of just waiting on our turn to say, *Amen.* Pa was the first to lower his head. Then Momma. Nelson and his company were gone. I lowered mine, peeking through my eyelashes. Pa's hand covered Momma's on the table. He set across from us. His big chest rose and lowered. The breath he let out told me that something was not right. Momma said her *Amen* aloud. Out of habit, I followed suit. Pa just opened his eyes, looking over at me. The Jazz in his glare was gone and replaced with the Blues.

"You won't be going to church today,"

I was saved! Only, I could not rejoice because they were still staring at me and something was obviously wrong. No church? How stupid would I be to smile at such news in front of Momma anyhow? "Why, Pa?"

"Your Grandmother thinks it is time for you to begin your etiquette and piano lessons," Momma answered for him.

I waited for more.

Momma continued, "She would like for you to stay with her for a few weeks,"

"'*A few weeks*'," I protested.

"'*A few weeks*'," the music was completely gone. Pa eyeballed me. It was a warning.

A few weeks did not sound too bad. Maybe she needed the company. Besides, Gran'ma Jordan was a teacher at church and at Booker T. Washington High School, which meant she lived on north Detroit with all the wealthy folks. Blocks away, closer to Deep Greenwood. Closer to Dreamland Theatre. Closer to my hiding spot to eavesdrop on folks. Learn how to read lips. But school? Longer walk, but school's almost over.

I smiled. "That's all right," I went for the bacon. When neither one of them spoke, I looked up chewing on a piece of crunchy goodness. They were looking at me like I grew a second nose and third ear. "What's wrong?"

Momma spoke first. "Now, you know your Grandmother makes

20

her own rules in her own home,"

"And you will respect those," Pa's eyes glared upward in my direction while his mouth went for the grits on his spoon.

"Yes, Sir,"

"Even if you do not believe them to be completely justifiable," Momma had not started eating.

Justice. *Justify. Justifiable.*

"Do you understand," Pa's voice was serious, but his eyes were dancing again.

"Yes, Sir," a smile tugged at my lips, but before it could spread, I jammed a fork full of eggs into my mouth. After chewing, I took my chance. "So, why is Gran'ma Jordan so, *mean*?" Pa avoided Momma's glare. It was his turn to stuff his mouth with food. These were the times when Pa was my ally. My ace. In silence. It was a question he could not ask.

"'*Mean*,' isn't quite the appropriate adjective, Honey," Momma shot another look at Pa. "She is just particular, that is all," Momma finally took a bite of bacon. "Which reminds me," she paused, ignoring Pa's smiling eyes. "Ellen cannot visit with you often. Neither can Jonathan. Only when you are here."

"What," my voice jumped a pitch too high.

Pa shot a glare in my direction. No sympathy in his eyes. There was no ally in disrespect.

"I apologize, but Momma—,"

"Her rules,"

"Momma," I was trying not to whine, but my throat did not get the message.

"Your tone,"

"Yes, Ma'am," I knew that was the end of it. Breakfast wasn't too good anymore.

"Finish your breakfast," Pa picked up his glass from the rim with one hand, set back in his seat. Finally, the sympathy returned. "It's only for three weeks," he took a gulp, glared some more. "You'll be leaving with your Grandmother after Wednesday's Bible study. You can handle it."

21

"Yes, Sir."

Pa was the only one going to church that morning. He was one of the trustees and had to be there to count the tithes and offerings at the end of service. He did not seem too bothered. He liked sticking around and talking to folks anyhow. On the church stairs, he kissed me on the forehead. He shifted to Momma, kissed her forehead. He moved closer to her ear away from my view. He whispered something. His hands rested on her waist. When he pulled back, she was smiling. Yuck. Of course, the kiss. Jazz and religion. Momma was always aware of my presence. Pa often seemed to forget. Or, maybe he did not know that I could see the tip of his tongue slip passed her lips. Disgusting.

Momma did not exactly explain where we were going that morning. In fact, when we returned to the taxicab, Momma did not say anything at all. Still, I waited for her to break the silence with an explanation. Instead, I was left with my own thoughts. Ray's Taxi Cab business never charged Momma or Pa. Mr. Ray was Pa's friend who moved to Tulsa from Mississippi. Ray, the owner, always made time to be the one to pick us up from church. It was the perfect time for him and Pa to catch up. It was actually Ray who I heard say one morning during their catching up that there was a Greenwood in Mississippi where he was from and that Greenwood Avenue here in Tulsa, Oklahoma had been named after it. This information, at the age of eight, made me ask a bunch of questions back then. Every street we passed, I would ask about its origin. "*Cincinnati*, Ohio," "*Detroit*, Michigan," "Migration of our people—well, in the US—from the wicked South to up North, which really ain't much different if it weren't for finding work," Mr. Ray would answer as I pointed to dusty signs. When Pa wasn't up for much talking, Momma and Pa would let me sit on the passenger side while they set in the back. This way, Mr. Ray could run his mouth to me. He was a talker who knew as much random information about the United States and other countries as the veterans did. Only, Mr. Ray was against war.

One ride to church, when the Negro veterans were returning to Tulsa in 1918, Mr. Ray had announced, "That son of yours may be silly over that gal, but he is smarter than he acts." Mr. Ray's belly had grown over the years and it was slightly hanging over his breeches then like it does now. The suspenders stretched with its curve. Momma had said nothing. Pa allowed the conversation to continue.

"Why do you say that, Mr. Ray," I pushed.

"He's smart enough not to fight in no war," and that was the end of it, maybe for Pa and Momma's sake. I wanted him to say more.

I liked Mr. Ray because he spoke to me like I was an adult. Even when I was not sure what he was talking about, he would continue to ramble long enough until I could figure it out myself. Well, most of whatever it was. A lot of adults were like Mr. Ray in Greenwood, but there was a fine line. I had to know who to talk to. Grown folks' business was grown folks' business. It was for me to know when it was and when it was not appropriate to ask many questions. In fact, the day Momma and I did not go to church, I knew not to ask anything. At least, not out loud. Yet. The ride down Greenwood and to the Depot was a quiet one. I observed as much as I could. I even noticed Momma clenching her jaw. A habit she picked up from Pa whenever he was bothered by something he could not control. Politics. Grown folks' business.

After waiting a while at the Depot, Momma's friend joined us in the cab. Back in town, again. Our reunion was a toothy greeting. All smiles and hugs. Mrs. Janette Wilson smelt like flowers. Not like they describe in books, but like real flowers. Like she could attract bees. Mrs. Wilson was from Texas and only came around when there was bad news. The year Momma was really sick and had to stay in bed for nearly two months, Mrs. Wilson showed up. The time Pa and Nelson had gotten into a real fight. The first and last time that would ever happen, but Mrs. Wilson was there. I can remember Mrs. Wilson supporting Momma who was unsure of whom to defend. Which makes me think about Nelson. We all knew then that there was something different about him, but that again, is another story Gran'ma Jordan would not see fit to discuss. After picking up Mrs. Wilson from the Depot, we ended up in the basement of another church. Last time when I joined Momma and Mrs. Wilson, I slept through most of a meeting they were having with folks. Considering I had just come from school, Momma let me doze off and did not wake me up until it was time to go.

"Have a seat, pay attention," she gestured towards a row of chairs in the front of the crowd while she and Mrs. Wilson spread their hellos.

Folks were happy to see them. I was sitting away from everyone else. I could not doze off in the front so I did as I was told and looked around. Tried to figure out what was about to happen. The church basement was set up like Vernon's. There were too many chairs to count separated by an aisle wide enough for elders who walked funny. There were old pictures of men in suits. There were no women in the pictures on the walls, but there was Jesus. The only white man and the largest picture. The congregation was full of women. I heard my voice grunt in my ears. I searched for someone my age and had no luck. I did not hear any kids chasing each other. No parents telling them not to run in the Lord's house, as if God himself was against it. The only thing I could hear was the hum of conversations. Whenever a group of women drew closer, the conversations would turn into a low whisper. Some of them stopped talking completely, said their hellos and moved on. When the last group of women took a seat on the opposite side of the room, I pushed myself up with the arms of the chair and stretched my neck. There had to be someone here I could talk to or else I was liable to make a fool out of myself by falling out of my chair from sleeping.

"Cross your legs, chil'," it was an order by a woman I recognized, but I could not remember her name. Her eyebrows were close together, lips tight. I never saw her sit on my side of the room. Two chairs were between us. "Yes, Ma'am," I did as I was told. My legs felt awkward and wobbly.

Momma stepped out of the crowd and walked in our direction. She was smiling at me, but something was still wrong. When she did not take a seat and stood in front of us, the humming of voices lowered and then completely vanished. Her left eyebrow rose. She was nervous. Only I knew this. For people watching, she probably appeared dignified and graceful. Focused. Serious. She took a breath. Her eyebrow lowered. In that same moment, she broke the silence. Her voice was strong, loud. The veins in her neck bounced against the surface of her smooth brown skin every time she spoke. I straightened my back, uncrossed my legs and crossed them at the ankles on the left side of my seat. I did not smile. I calculated my blinking. Maybe I looked as passionate as she did. Maybe I looked constipated. I relaxed, but nodded and let out a low shout whenever the other ladies shouted much louder. I held Momma's stare on occasions, pretending like I knew exactly what she was going to say next.

Momma's eyes lingered in my direction. "I do not want my baby growing up in a world where she will assume it is all right to be beaten down," the crowd agreed. "Beaten, lynched and burned." The crowd rocked. Screamed. I heard an *Amen* somewhere in the back, to my right. A woman shouted something in anger before Momma could continue. This time, I kept quiet. Scanned the crowd. "Mary Turner, eight months pregnant, was killed after watching her husband beaten and lynched. Murdered by a white mob. The both of'em," I did not know Mary Turner, but I knew she did not live in Tulsa. Wherever she lived, it might as well have happened here. Momma was furious. *Lynched? While pregnant?* "We will not allow such disgusting dehumanization to happen here . . ." *Human. De-human-i-za-tion.* ". . . To our families. To our communities. They will not humiliate us in efforts to keep us in our place! Our place on this God given Earth is no different from their own!"

Our place.

Chapter Five
Trouble

That night, I tracked the dark ceiling in my room. Thinking. Thinking about how White folks called our side of town *"Little Africa"* and about how those words meant something different for us when we said it. It felt dirty coming out of Pigtail's mouth. Like something was wrong with Greenwood. Like something was wrong with me. Then, I thought about Mrs. Mary Turner. Her, her husband and her baby that were on the other side of the country. What was wrong with them? Then about going to Gran'ma Jordan's. What was so wrong that I had to move in with her on the other side of Greenwood? Or, what was wrong with me? If there was something wrong, what was right?

I would be closer to Deep Greenwood. Which, could mean one or two things. Trouble would either find me or I would find it. That's what I heard Momma warn Pa when they thought I was sleeping. When their voices grew too low to hear, I listened for something else.

There was a train in the distance. Lying in bed, Deep Greenwood felt mysterious. I wondered who was getting on and off the trains. I imagined that I could hear the hum of movement down there if I stayed up long enough. The same movement during the day, only caught in the night. The first image that replaced the darkness was a crowd of men and women smiling under the moonlight. The second, children my age dancing under the street lights. Pretending like most of us did not have to be in bed at a decent hour. My imagination did not stop there. It listened in on forbidden conversations between bellhops and porters making deals with patrons while white prostitutes set patiently in elegant hotel rooms expecting their victims. Jazz, a religious woman's enemy, whined in the background. Shining shoes, thanks to well-tipped shoeblacks, slid across a wooden floor. Women's dresses twirl too high for Momma's liking, but the thoughts in Pa's eyes continued to dance. Nelson stood in a dark corner. Broad shoulders. Thick neck and big head. A homemade jacket and trousers clung to his masculine build. He peeks at his pocket watch. Back home, Momma clutched her Bible. Pa retreated to his office to write and Nelson never returned.

Nelson was the kind of man I heard about in the 'papers. He stood in dark areas of Jazz and pool halls making jokes to entertain the people. He was clever. They laughed uncontrollably. Enemies were unable to resist the urge. He could influence crowds. Discuss politics. He was also brave. A man who would die protecting his family from the Klan. He was a hero. That was my imagination. In reality, he was a boy goofy over some girl named Beatrice. For her, he would do anything. Sometimes, it came with a price. I suppose that meant he was still a hero to someone.

There was a pop. More like a *bang*. It vibrated. I vibrated. All in my head. A gun. On Archer. The Depot. There was no real threat. Gunshots were common the closer we got to summer. In most cases, the barrel of the gun is pointed up to the sky and the trigger pulled only to scare off an enemy. Archer attracted activities we—kids—weren't supposed to know about. I knew, from eavesdropping on Nelson, that Archer was the entryway for Greenwood to have more than Negro patrons. Just as many Whites come down to Deep Greenwood from Archer as Negroes did. The fancy oil men too. Nelson called Archer the Red Light District, but a name like that seemed more appropriate for night. This is how I learned about the prostitutes.

Beatrice was strange.

Strange in that mysterious non-motherly kind of way. During the day, she wore silk dresses, big hats and gloves. Her body was slim, but her hips curved like they were meant for more fat. During the day, she smoked cigarettes. Her breath smelt like tea and tobacco. Tea was her habit after supper. As beautiful as she was, the makeup made her look worn and tired. Without it, her cheekbones seemed to set higher, fuller. She was nothing like the woman at the Depot. I closed my eyes, pushing back my memory. *She was a short woman, but somehow stood tall. Serious eyes . . . A.C. Freeman. He walked boldly toward them. He seemed taller; more like Pa and not like my big-headed brother Nelson. Balanced shoulders. His hat lowered to his chest. His free hand extended out to her.*

I opened my eyes with the moonlight. It danced alongside the shadows of tree branches across my bedroom ceiling. What was I going to do at Gran'ma Jordan's? This was home. Home, for the four of us, was a quiet three-bedroom rectangle with a porch, living room, one bathroom and a kitchen. The kitchen had an awkward corner for the circular dining room table that somehow stood comfortably in both the living room and kitchen. Without a paved street, rainy days guaranteed mud puddles to wrap around our porch and boots. It rained in the afternoon the day before. The puddles were still there. I heard them come in. Nelson and Beatrice. I would have to clean the floors tomorrow. Our house was usually quiet and clean, until they strolled in. Late. There was the sound of the pots. Laughing and giggling for a while as they stole a piece of happiness. Danced with it. Flirted with it. Next, the cursing. He did most of the talking. She struggled with her words until they were accompanied with desperate tears. Lastly, the bitter sounds of a man and woman struggling. The expected smack of a hand striking flesh. Happiness dissolved and exposed two strangers. If Momma and Pa ever heard, we never knew. They never interfered. The struggle ended with stumbling feet and boots passing my bedroom. A door would click shut. The jammed lock. The crying. Or giggling?

In the morning, Beatrice would be sitting at the table. A bruised lip holding on to a cigarette, but she would smile. Momma would hum Pa's tune in the kitchen, making breakfast. I would try not to stare, but I will glance too often. Beatrice will hold her smile, but her eyes would not. I want to ask a question, but it is not my place. So I ask another. I make sure to smile. "What do you see when you look around?"

Beatrice glared off. Like she's thinking about it.

But she never answers.

Chapter Six
More Trouble

"Why did Pastor Freeman's son go to jail?"

They exchanged glances. Smaller eyes avoided looking in my direction. The elders set there staring at me like I said something wrong. Like I had looked them in the eyes and told them that I did not believe in God. Like they were waiting on me to get struck by lightning. No fear, just expecting stares like they always gave whenever I asked a question they were too religious to answer. He did not come to church. Had not seen him since the Depot, so I figured I would just ask them about him.

Church folk were like the folks who were wealthy enough to stroll into Dreamland or the Dixie Theatre smiling real big so long as they have the pleasure of believing in something that made them feel better about the world. I started feeling this way at Bible Study and Sunday School because of elders who pushed the name of God around on people who were younger than them. Or pushed God on people who were worse sinners, in their opinion. Oh, I believed in God, but not in the ways that some old folk spoke about Him.

"What does Pastor Freeman's son having to go to jail have anything to do with today's lesson?"

"Well," Ellen was speaking in my defense. I listened, already amused. "Today's lesson is about Jesus being punished for simply trying to save the world—,"

"Ellen,"

"From what I hear, Mr. A. C. Freeman got himself into some trouble up in Chi—,"

"Ellen,"

The smile on Ellen's face relaxed, words stopped and she cut her eyes in my direction. She tried. We exchanged a smile.

"It is not appropriate to discuss the First Family's business. I'll be speaking with Sister Jordan about your curiosity. I hear that you will be joining her this Wednesday."

It was not a question. She already knew for certain. So, we couldn't speak about the First Family's business, but we could speak about mine?

At school, during lunch, we snuck out of Dunbar and headed for Dreamland or Dixie Theatre on Greenwood. Whichever one we could make it to first without getting caught. As we waited for a taxi, I listened in to two men talking near Pete's Jewelry store where Momma sold the pieces she made.

"Cancelled stamp, that's what she is. A wurp,"

"Unless she get ahold of a lil' giggle water,"

Both men laughed.

"What's a wurp," I whispered the question to Ellen and John-Jon.

"I don't know. Let's go!"

This could be the last time, so we wanted to make it mean something. Jumping on the back of a taxicab, Ellen, John-Jon and I would hang on for as long as we weren't discovered. Which, did not take too long because it was not completely normal to have three kids hanging off a taxi. Ellen always looked like she was in pain while John-Jon and I held on as if it were the proper way to ride a taxi. I could have just asked Mr. Ray or his workers for a normal ride to Deep Greenwood without having to cover the pay, but jumping a taxicab as a trio was far more interesting. Besides, Momma always say I needed more exercise. Depending on who was driving, turning corners and bumping curbs could come with a few scraped knees if we did not use most of our strength to hang on. Momma would not be too happy to see that. A scraped knee usually meant no stockings and she knew how much Gran'ma Jordan despised me coming to church with no stockings. It just wasn't proper, especially at church.

Church.

"Let's jump off up there," I shielded my eyes from the sun, narrowed in on the new building being built for Vernon.

"Where," Ellen's voice caught in the wind. I watched her left foot slip. The tail of her dress wrapped around her right ankle. She tightened her grip. For her, the sooner we were off, the better.

"The church," I pointed with my chin.

"Why," John-Jon grunted, squinting. His body remained pressed against the opposite hip of the cab. "Let's take it down to Dreamland,"

The steel was hard under my fingers. Warm and hard. The sun was hot. Really, really hot. My body had that feeling like drinking warm soup in the summer. Today, the weather decided to beat the cold. The church passed by behind John-Jon. We missed our chance.

"Guys, let's get off,"

We looked at Ellen. She had her hair pressed and straightened today. I always knew when her Pa was able to get back on his feet because he would be sure to get Ellen's hair done for her. Before getting on the cab, her hair had fallen down her back. Now, it was big and bushy. Its length had shrunk to her shoulders. I kind of liked it there, but I don't think she did.

The cab bucked over loose gravel. "One," I started.

"Two," John-Jon sounded disappointed.

Ellen did not finish. Instead, she jumped off before completing the count. The tail of her dress flew after her. She did not relax her body and tried to catch her fall. I saw it before it happened. Her right leg bent under her body right before she fell back on the ground. I jumped after her. In the same moment, the sound of tires scraping against gravel came from our right. A loud screeching sound was coming from Ellen. She was wide-eyed and motionless.

"Stay there," I stopped her from sitting up as soon as she tried to move.

"It hurts!"

"What hurts," John-Jon appeared on her right side. "Ellen, what happened?"

"What were you doing on the back of that Taxi," Jim, one of Mr. Ray's drivers, lowered himself to the ground near John-Jon.

"Is it broke! Is it broke? Tell me it's not broken!"

"Ellen, calm down," I wasn't the one with my leg jammed nearly underneath my body, but I did not want her to freak out either. We were causing a scene. Jim had pulled over in the middle of the road. A crowd appeared out of nowhere along the road on either side.

"Was she hit?"

"Did she fall?"

"How?"

Voices were flooding around us.

"Why were you on the back of the taxi," Jim was in just as much shock as Ellen. He was screaming, but I don't think he realized it. His eyebrows were close together. His mouth twisted. "I don' told y'all about getting on the back–,"

"Jim," Mr. Lawrence Freeman appeared between him and John-Jon. I had not realized that he had ever been around. Up close, he resembled his younger brother, A.C. I suddenly felt like a child. Embarrassed, but I could not look away. He held Jim's gaze. Jim's face relaxed. They both searched downward where Ellen was lying. I watched him. "Do you think you can stand up," it was a question, but it did not sound like one. His face was so relaxed.

Ellen was crying and breathing heavy now, "I . . . don't know,"

"How's your left leg," his hand wrapped around her waist, supporting her. I grabbed her left hand, but it seemed useless. She must have thought the same, because her hand slipped from mine and her arm swung around my neck. Her body hung. Supporting herself on her left leg and my neck, she was heavy. Heavy and wobbly. I searched for John-Jon. Squinting my eyes against the sun, I found him standing back with Jim. His eyes were lowered on Ellen's leg. Her knee was bent, her leg stretched out behind her. She strained to keep her foot from lowering to the ground.

"Is anything else hurt?" Mr. Lawrence straightened to his full length. Ellen's weight shifted. I held on to her, but relaxed a little.

She sniffed. "My foot,"

"Your foot and what part of your leg?"

"My ankle and my knee," she winced. Her arm coiled from around my neck and raised the tail of her dress. Her stockings were ruined and stained above her knee. I glanced at Mr. Lawrence while he examined her leg. I grew embarrassed for her. Skin was peeled and exposed a lighter shade. A shallow layer of blood returned to its surface just as we were looking at it.

"They were on the back of the cab," Jim accused, looking over at John-Jon, Ellen and I. His mouth still twisted. "I don' told them that that there is dangerous. She lucky a busted ankle and scraped knee is all she

32

got!"

"Jim, I'll take care of it from here," Mr. Lawrence bent down, picking Ellen up completely off the ground. With the swift movement, I smelt the scent that followed him. She let go of me completely and wrapped both of her arms around his neck. If it were not inappropriate and bad timing, I would have asked about the whereabouts of his brother.

Ellen's legs dangled over his left arm. To my surprise, she did not look awkward in his arms. She was tall and from an odd angle she could get away with looking like his lover who had been swept off her feet. The thought made me feel weird. All that for a scratch and a twisted ankle.

She wasn't that hurt, but she was hurt enough to get us all in trouble. That gave reason for Momma and Pa to make it clear that I was not to give Gran'ma Jordan any trouble about wanting to be with John-Jon and Ellen. I was not to leave Gran'ma's house unless it were for returning home, church or to go to school.

Well, at least I still had school to look forward to. Then, the summer.

Chapter Seven
Second Coming

A book isn't just for reading. Lemons are not just for lemonade. Fingers could be shaped. Maybe even a nose. Gran'ma Jordan introduced all of this to me that made me wonder where all these etiquette remedies came from. Who would have thought putting a lemon on my elbows and knees would keep them from getting black? The book. The book on top of my head wobbles and falls to the ground every time; exposing me.

"Stand tall. Back straight. Stomach in,"

Tall. Straight. Almost. Stomach?

It fell again. I twisted my body and leaned in to catch it. The book slipped through my fingers and knees. "Can I take a break?"

Her throat cleared.

"Ma'am," I corrected.

She did not say yes and she did not say no. She just walked away towards the kitchen. Later, she went off to take care of some business outside of the bungalow.

I was left reading The Story of Doctor Dolittle about some guy who becomes a veterinarian after he learns to speak with animals. Travels to Africa with animals. I stopped reading whenever it got weird and included some African prince who wished he were white so that he could marry a sleeping beauty. Learned it was no story of my liking. I put the book aside and decided to see what was really going on out in the world. Gran'ma Jordan would be out for a while. It seemed to be her routine.

I found myself walking to the tracks thinking about Doctor Dolittle and the Prince. Why did the Prince have to be white to get the Sleeping Beauty? I stopped near the tracks and waited. I waited for them until I was bored. Blue Eyes never showed and neither did his disciples. I thought they would. Though, somewhere inside of me was happy that they did not. At least not while I was alone. There was something about white people that was scary like that. Well, not scary. Just weird. It was always like they were thinking things their mouths would not say aloud. Unless they were Blue Eyes. He was nothing like the folks who came by Pa's store looking for things.

They would talk to Pa like he was one of them, but their eyes were a little shifty. Before leaving with whatever materials they were looking to purchase or something Pa convinced them that they needed, they would talk for a while like passing neighbors all friendly-like. White folks seemed friendly, but sometimes you could catch them looking like they were holding on to judgments they would never say aloud. Well, except for a guy that was reminded by his wife's uncomfortable, silent gaze that Pa was a Negro. Her pointy nose towards the ceiling. Some of their children ran around the store no matter what their mother told them not to do. It was odd to me that the same mother who could not get a handle on her children looked so mean. Well, she did not only look mean. With every glance in Pa's direction there was a question there in her expression. A question that challenged Pa's trustworthiness. Like whatever Pa was selling was not worth its price. Pa just kept on talking like he never noticed it. Never went down on his prices. Never addressed the question in their eyes. Her cold stares somehow became her husband's after he would look her way. Eventually, they would buy and go on about their way. Sure enough, in a month's time, that customer would be back. Without his wife and kids. Pa's customers always came back. That's why when I saw A.C. Freeman enter the store one afternoon, I knew he was up to something that would make him come back. Or, at least, I hoped so.

He was so quick about his business. In and out. Unfortunately, Pa was not up for much talking because he had to get somewhere on the other side of Greenwood. Said it was important. Was going to get me home to Gran'ma Jordan and then be on his way. That was a couple of days ago. Now, another day with Pa, I waited for him. I watched customers come and go. Though I was living with Gran'ma Jordan, I was spending most of my time with Pa in the Glass House. I was hoping A.C. would be back. When he never came after a couple of hours passed, I told Pa I was heading back to Gran'ma Jordan's for piano lessons. Of course, I did not quite go straight to Gran'ma's after leaving the Glass House. I found a spot near the Depot and started my search.

I watched Mr. Lawrence. Other than being Pastor's eldest son, Mr. Lawrence was a bellhop for Hector's Hotel. I did not know Hector personally. All I knew was that he was a short, stocky man with creepy eyes who wore loose trousers and overcoats a size too small. Hector never spoke to children, but he wasn't that interesting to us either. I watched the commotion. Hector was probably inside. I watched Mr. Lawrence, hoping that he was waiting near the entrance for his brother. Mr. Lawrence and A.C. had a sister named Marie Freeman. She was one of those women you did not see much unless it was either in church or her garden at their bungalow on Detroit not too far from Gran'ma Jordan's. I wondered why I had not seen her much. I suspected that Mr. Lawrence would not be waiting for her. He could just be standing there doing his job like he was doing whenever Ellen busted her knee, but I was hopeful. Hoping A.C. would show up and meet him standing there. I wanted to know what happened in Chicago from A.C. himself and was planning to ask as soon as I got the chance. Asking Momma and Pa did not go anywhere. At church, Momma dismissed the question like I had asked if the sun had fallen out of the sky. They had other things occupying their minds or were too busy trying to keep me out of adult's business. I told myself that I would just wait. Wait and find out, today. Catch up to him and talk to him like I did back in the day.

I watched Mr. Lawrence. He was just standing there. The crowd was patient. He tipped his hat, allowing other bellhops to take care of arriving guests. They did not seem bothered. I let my feet dangle from the wagon. The morning rain had cooled the weather. Men and families walked by me with smiles on their faces. Some tipped their hats while others inquired about my parents and Nelson. It did not take long for me to be discovered by Ellen and John-Jon. They came running up to my sanctuary. Both were sweating and struggled to pull themselves up on the wagon. A coat of sweat brought a shine to John-Jon's black forehead. I smiled to myself. He sure did have a huge head.

"I thought we were supposed to meet near the taxis? We could steal a ride on the back and go down to Dreamland," Ellen smiled. "My ankle is better,"

"Not today," I strained my neck. Pushing up on both knees, I scanned the crowd in front of Hector's Hotel. Got so distracted by John-Jon's glistening forehead that I nearly forgot what I was doing. I strained some more.

John-Jon's head popped in my view again. "Why not,"

"I have business," I shoved him.

"*Business*," he regrouped, lowered a leg over the wagon's edge and pulled his scarred knee to his chest. His right knee was always the knee with scars. It was the same knee that hit the ground first when I dared him to jump out of Gran'ma Dee's, Pa's mother, big tree in hot Louisiana. As a result of it, that was John-Jon's first and last visit for the summers.

"You too young for business," Ellen chimed in, relaxing against the wood to our left.

"Maybe y'all are, but I'm not,"

"What *business*,"

"A.C.," she grinned.

I rolled my eyes.

"Every time she got ahold of the *Tulsa Star* she used to look for an article on him," Ellen fluttered her eyelashes. "She has a crush,"

"Oooooh," John-Jon grinned, but his eyes looked uninterested.

"If you knew any better, you would know that he's been to jail,"

"So," John-Jon frowned.

Ellen was still smiling, teasing me.

"The son of Pastor Freeman went to jail," I tried to explain for the second time. More serious.

"So," John-Jon shrugged.

"I'm going to find out why," I put my eyes back on Hector's Hotel.

"What makes you think he's coming there?"

"Ellen, there's his brother," I exhaled, exaggerating my irritation.

"So,"

"Is that the only word you know," I glared at the side of John-Jon's face. He sucked spit through his teeth.

"How long you plan on sitting here,"

"As long as it takes,"

"Why,"

"Why not," I looked over at Ellen. "Have something more

interesting to do?" She scanned the crowds. "Let's go beat up the Carlton kids,"

"Not today," I shook my head. They groaned.

"What makes you think he's going to tell you why anyway?"

"He will,"

"He won't,"

"He will," I glared at John-Jon, waiting on him to challenge me again. He grew bored and lowered his knee. Both of his feet dangled next to mine. I was sitting diagonally across from him, twisted with my back against the same wood frame as Ellen was leaning on. Both of her knees cradled her flat chest. We set like that for a while. Ellen was the first to break the silence.

"I can't wait for school Monday. This weekend is too long," Ellen complained.

"I can, today is just a boring day because of her,"

I nudged John-Jon with my right foot. They laughed.

"Can we find something else to do," Ellen begged.

"Like what," I watched her search the sky.

Her eye sockets stretched like she was suddenly hit with a message from God.

"Let's go spy on someone,"

"On who," John-Jon and I asked the same question.

"Ooooon," she paused, then grinned from me to John-Jon to me again. "*Beatrice*?"

"Beatrice," John-Jon strained his face.

"That's that weird woman who stay with her," Ellen reminded him.

I shook my head at both of them. "No good,"

"Then who," John-Jon's eyes danced.

"On her," I spotted her immediately.

The heavy fedora. Trousers, the boots. The same suitcases. She walked with her chin high, eyes skimming faces and buildings. She walked sideways in the crowd. Her lips moved. I read them. She was excusing herself.

"Who is she? I ain't never seen't her before,"

I scrambled to my feet. I stretched my neck, keeping my eye on her cutting through the crowds. "She met him at the Depot. Maybe she's meeting him again,"

"Who is *she* and who did *she* meet?" John-Jon stood next to me. He was about three inches taller. For that, I slapped his shoulder, forcing him to move. He stepped back.

"Where'd she go?" I jumped from the wagon.

Ellen and John-Jon stayed on my heels. I filled them in through breaths. "Lawrence introduced her to A.C.," I glanced over my shoulder. They were listening. I slowed down and whispered.

"Let's spy on her."

Chapter Eight
Womanhood?

I was unsure about a lot of things. I did not know much about what it meant to be a man or a *proper* woman, but I knew enough about Nelson and Beatrice to know when something's wrong between a man and a woman. My gut felt like there was something I needed to know about her. Her and the Pastor's sons.

We followed her to Deep Greenwood. She would stop occasionally. When it was John-Jon's turn to linger close enough, he found out she was looking for rooms for rent. Rent. She was young, with no husband. Up close, I stood next to Ronald's Bar-B-Q pretending to be interested in the menu near the door. I heard her speak. Her voice is like a woman's and not as young as she looks. Soft, inviting. She asked one of the waiters how much to rent a room. They spoke briefly and she was on her way back out the door. I glanced over at Ellen standing next to John-Jon across the paved street. They were distracted, talking. Glanced in my direction. I took steps forward, they followed suit.

The woman came to a stop in front of Helen's Beauty Shop. Another eavesdropping sanctuary. I turned my left hip toward her, glancing in her direction. She looked up at the brick building, searched. There was no sign. Donna Webster, a woman known for few words, stood in the entrance of the shop. She spoke, but Donna did not return her greeting. Finally, she extended a hand. Donna took it, but she did not seem impressed. I truly needed to learn to read lips. In a short exchange of words, they were both headed inside the shop. I waved to John-Jon and Ellen warning them not to follow me. They hesitated, pouted and then remained where they were across the street. I entered the shop, making immediate contact with Sister Helen. She stood under praying hands placed carefully on the wall near her station. Sister Hannah, a woman with big eyes and a goofy expression, was sitting in the chair in front of her. I greeted both of them with hellos and a hug. Turning to the other women, I offered them hugs and said my good afternoons before taking a seat near the back. I waved, offering *her* a shaky smile. She looked at me suspiciously, but said hello anyway. Her smile was honest. I had been caught staring too long. In efforts to save myself the embarrassment, I grabbed a newspaper and pretended to be more interested in Sister Helen. I made sure to only look in Sister Helen's direction whenever the women spoke.

" . . . Whites are afraid,"

"Of what, Sister Helen,"

"They think they're losing control of *their* city. My daughter got her hands on that ole *Tulsa Tribune* newspaper. Said something about concentration camps, concentration camps for the *IWW* and other pro-Hun individuals - their words. Said they should 'leave the country'," she grunted, shaking her head.

Sister Ethel, who was sitting next to me further away from the door in the row of only three seats, mouthed the words Industrial Workers of the World. I thought about Jess' Semple who had seen the note on the pole near the Depot the day the woman and A.C. showed up. Reading lips wasn't too bad, up close. I nodded my understanding, but I was still confused.

"The Knights of Liberty,"

"You mean the Ku Klux Klan,"

"*Patriotism* at its finest,"

"No, *Christianity* at its best,"

"Can't believe that they really think they're doing the Lord's work!"

The women laughed. It grew serious in a matter of seconds. Sister Helen spoke with a trained tongue. "The chief of police was there the night of the beating. There's no action against the vigilantes. That bombing was staged. Used to target the IWW and get rid of their hall on Brady Street,"

"All that has nothing to do with us here in Greenwood. They exclude us from the oil fields. We—,"

"Don't speak too soon, Sister James," she pointed the end of the comb in the direction of Mrs. James sitting next to the woman I followed inside. I stole a glance at her. She was watching Sister Helen closely, waiting. "That oil money comes through Greenwood just as much as it does white Tulsa. My daughter works for a family out South. When she

41

comes home on Sunday, she only spends her wages right here," the comb pointed down at the wooden floor. "Not to mention the white men who come dancing, gambling, drinking, and carrying on—on Archer Street and Deep Greenwood doing God knows what. Let's just call it 'pursuing ungodly pleasures'."

While the women laughed, I watched *her*. She looked focused, like Father. A smile tugged at her lips, but it wasn't convincing anymore. She was here, but her mind was elsewhere. A sudden burst of laughter brought my attention back on the other women. I listened carefully, hoping for more, but the spirit of the conversation shifted. Sister Helen and the seven others exchanged information on programs for churches, family updates and gossip that wasn't interesting enough to care about. When the sun was heavy in the sky, Donna, who had been standing near the door outside, finally spoke. She stepped away from the wall near the entrance of the parlor. Sunrays planted kisses across her golden face. That's when I noticed Ellen and John-Jon's absence across the road. I had forgotten all about the two of them.

Gran'ma Jordan would be worried, but I did not mind. Besides, I had Sister Helen as my saving grace.

"Sister Helen, I am going to head home," Donna was exhausted. I had seen her a few times in Sister Helen's shop. Just sitting. Never getting her hair done. She was a frail woman that wasn't seen much, but everyone knew her daughter. Her daughter was a friend of Beatrice, Nelson's muse.

"I am sorry Florence has not returned,"

She didn't acknowledge the apology. "You are welcome to offer her room to this young lady," her eyes lowered. I followed her gaze down on the woman I followed. "She is new in town and in need of a place to stay."

Helen nodded, but I sensed she had already been suspecting this to happen. Embracing Donna, she whispered something near her ear and escorted her out the door. When Helen returned, there was sympathy in her eyes.

"I am Helen Burnett, the owner of this fine establishment," she smiled. The women laughed. I smiled. *Ownership*. "My husband owns the grocer across the road and the insurance company next door," she was proud, "You are,"

The woman rose to her feet. "Edith Franklin,"

Edith Franklin.

"It is nice to meet you, Darling. Put that hand down. We are not afraid to hug around here. Grab your trunk; I'll take the other. Follow me," to my surprise, Sister Helen looked over her shoulder at me; stopping the both of them from heading upstairs. "Are you here to help sweep for me?"

"I—," I hadn't planned on it, but I needed the excuse.

"I can put you to work. Take you home later. It's near the summer anyhow; you kids need some work to do. I'll be back down with a broom."

I did not protest.

Sweeping like pouring molasses, I watched Edith standing in the entrance. She had returned downstairs from being upstairs for a while. The door was open, allowing in a spring breeze. She was looking out toward a Model T Ford that was parked in front of the opposite red brick buildings housing the grocer and pool hall. People swarmed from every direction. Kids ran down the road heading toward the YMCA and Dixie Theatre. I did not see Ellen nor John-Jon, but in the midst of the crowds, I noticed him immediately. We noticed him. He was easy to notice.

He walked with pride. A smile added a layer of humility to his expression. He greeted those who greeted him, exchanging small conversations until he shifted his direction toward the motorcar. A woman wearing an oversized Gage hat and silk dress approached him. They had to be involved beyond acquaintance in private spaces. Their bodies were close. Her skilled hand removed his fedora from his head and pressed it against his chest as if reminding him of courtesy. His palm covered her small hand in the split second it took her to remove it. Words were spoken. He was smiling. His head shifted, eyes searched to his left. Lowering my head, I stole a quick glance at Edith. She was turning her back to them, walking deeper into the parlor. I swept closer near the stairs, keeping my eyes on the floor for a moment.

"As soon as I am done here, I will do something to that hair. How's a good washing," Helen was looking over at Edith.

"I truly appreciate your generosity, Mrs. Burnett, but I do not have the cash. I would feel much better if I were able to pay you for your services,"

"Please, call me Sister Helen," she stopped combing. "It was not a question. Take a seat, I will start on you soon," she winked.

Edith smiled. "Truly indebted, Sister Helen,"

"My pleasure, Darling,"

Edith took the seat where she had been when first arriving. Before the women could continue their conversation, the silk dress danced into the parlor. A full mouth of pearly whites outlined by a smile of full lips. Eyes that danced to attract the weakness of men, cat-shaped. High cheekbones and thin eyebrows enhanced with makeup. She was beautiful. Young. The four ladies greeted her warmly. She offered them all dainty hellos and small talk, settling her attention on Sister Helen.

"You hear about any jobs south," a smirk was on Sister Helen's lips.

"There's some families looking for help, as usual," she answered.

"Find out about any unusual work from Lawrence?" Sister Helen's mention of Mr. Lawrence's name brought an elephant in the room. It stood in the corner near Helen struggling not to be seen.

"My mother has been here, I presume,"

"Yes, she has given your room to this young lady, Edith,"

The elephant tiptoed across the wooden floor and set next to her. Florence looked her from toe-to-head. No smile, but seemingly in the same motion, she grinned.

"She is new in town. Where'd you say you were from, Darling?"

Edith had never shared this information with Sister Helen. Nor had anyone asked until now. I listened. "Boley, Oklahoma,"

"Boley, huh," Florence gracefully divided the breeze and took a seat next to her. The elephant vanishes. "Got tired of the rural air, huh,"

"Used to be more refreshing,"

Florence hummed, uninterested. "I will return to retrieve some of my things from upstairs," she stood. "In a few hours. Do be here, I would hate to accidentally leave with some of your belongings," Florence grinned and disappeared out of the parlor.

I had taken a break from sweeping when Florence returned. I

picked up the broom with more zeal. Completing the task with more motivation, I dashed off to put the broom away. Ascending the stairs, I slowed down whenever I noticed the door upstairs was halfway open.

I came to a stop and peaked through the crack. By now, Edith was awake from a nap she decided to take earlier. She was sitting up. Her feet planted on the floor. She stayed quiet on the edge of the bed watching Florence. From a drawer, Florence pulled out a stocking. Slipping a hand inside of its limp mouth, a folded stack of bills came out with her fist.

"When did you get in town," Florence asked. "Recently,"

"Where have you been staying?"

"I've been managing,"

"Looking for a job,"

"Yes,"

"Two options," she counted the money, stuffed it down her dress. "North or South," Edith didn't answer soon enough. Florence repeated, "North or South?"

"North,"

"Good choice," she came to stand in front of her, invading her space. "You don't look like you're made for a maid's work." Her hand pinched Edith's chin, jerked her head upward. Examined her. "There was a Negro woman in Wagoner some years ago who was dragged through the streets. Hauled her right down the Main Street for killing a white man who would not give her what she was due. Won't have to worry too much about that kind of thing happening here. It may seem like white women get paid more, but as many times their husbands come down to Archer, we get triple,"

"We? Triple?"

She twisted her mouth, waited.

Edith nodded.

Florence laughed. Her hand slipped from her chin. "Nineteen... Twenty?"

"Close,"

She was searching for something. Turning her back to us, she pulled out the drawers to a small dresser. "How many men,"

"Excuse me,"

She stopped, stood straight. Watching Edith, she laughed again. "Forgive me,"

"I have never been a prostitute,"

"You don't have to be a prostitute to be with a man," her laugh was replaced with a smile. "Something tells me you already know that," Florence waited.

"Not exactly,"

Florence's eyes narrowed, her expression was still playful. I grew uncomfortable for Edith's sake. Florence laughed. "You finish schooling?"

"Yes,"

"Who is he?"

"Excuse me,"

"You are not a virgin,"

"What," Edith remained calm, but she seemed insulted.

"Do I offend you," Florence's question was sincere.

"No, your questions are just—that's where you get the money,"

Florence hummed, went back to searching.

"Sister Helen mentioned a gentleman named Lawrence," Edith pressed. She was pretending she had not met him at the Depot. I watched Florence. She was hesitant. The humming lowered. Edith had her attention. "The ladies do not seem too fond of him,"

Florence glared over her exposed right shoulder. "Where are your belongings?"

Edith glanced back at the suitcases near the bed. I moved closer to the door and held my breath. Florence scanned them, turned her gaze back in front of her and returned to humming. "How many people have you met since your arrival," the question briefly interrupted her rhythm.

"Not many, stumbled across this parlor after seeing your mother standing near the door. If you don't mind me asking—,"

"I-do," Florence snapped. Within seconds, she continued humming.

"What do y'all do for fun around here," Edith sounded amused.

Florence's high spirits returned. She stood straight, stretched and twirled. Hands in the air, head high and eyes closed.

She sung, "Do you own a silk dress?"

Chapter Ten
Manhood?

"Ma, let's go!"

"Don't rush me, chil'. You have never been this excited to go to church. What has gotten into you?"

"The Holy Ghost," We laughed, but she covered her smile because she did not usually participate in joking about God. It felt good to see her relax.

"Pleeeeeease, come on,"

"Waiting on that father of yours,"

I pouted, flopping down on the sofa. Momma shook her head, smiling and ignoring my impatience. Her eyes narrowed. I caught her warning, crossing my legs. I had a ruin in my left stocking. Tugging at the tail of my ruffled dress, I covered my thigh and the sheer tear. Momma smiled, probably proud that the time with Gran'ma Jordan's seemed to be useful. After the first week, I was allowed to spend the weekend with Momma and Pa. It felt good returning to our morning routine, together. The house felt new. Though, it felt much smaller having been in Gran'ma's massive bungalow. Momma slipped on her white gloves. They looked new. Through her spread fingers, I could see the bookshelf Pa made in my time of being gone. Momma decorated it with six white glass doves. The doves held the books in place. The shelf was new, the books I had already read two summers ago. On top of the bookshelf were Momma's three flower pots. It was the perfect spot. In the morning, the sun blinked and stretched across the room in a bright ray of light hitting the petals. This morning was no different. By noon, the summer sun would be wide awake and burning the face of whoever dared to stand in front of the window with the curtains open. Momma wiggled her fingers. I focused on her, meeting her gaze and smile. Pa came strolling in the living room wearing his second handmade suit. The dark trousers were loose closer to the ankle. The jacket fit over his shoulders and rounded with his torso. He was tall, strong.

"Did I hear my Bumpkin Head getting excited about Sunday school?"

I smiled up at him. "Good morning, Pa,"

I was Pa's favorite. He has never told me that, but it is what I believed. Momma never seemed too bothered. Besides, she had Nelson to look after and protect. Jumping up, I ran into his arms. His hands wrapped under my armpits and swung me up from the ground. I clasped my hands behind his neck, legs around his waist and accepted his kiss on my forehead. With Gran'ma Jordan and with Momma, it was easy to feel the responsibility of being older. With Pa, I was still a big baby and I loved the feeling it gave me from time-to-time.

"You're getting taller, Bumpkin Head,"

"You're getting too old for that," Momma's voice was calm. "Keep your feet on the ground, Honey."

Pa gave me one last kiss on the forehead before I slid to the floor. He stepped in Momma's direction, placed his hand on her lower back and pecked her on the cheek. Tilting his head, he whispered something in her ear. She smiled. I waited. With a laugh in her throat, she held her gloved palm out to me. Glancing from him to her, I slipped my hand into hers. He walked to the door and opened it like a bellhop. One hand behind his back while the other glided through the air escorting us out the door. "Ladies first," his right eye winked while the other gazed at Momma. A smile was on his lips. This wasn't anything new. They were always whispering or saying something to each other with their bodies. Of course whenever they did not want me to hear anything specific. That sure didn't make me feel like I was *getting too old*. Sometimes, they made me feel like a baby. Not how Pa made me feel, but a baby like I was too young for them to say certain things around. Sure, adults' business is *adults' business*, but why treat me like an adult and a child in the same instance? I knew more about a lot than they suspected. Take Nelson and Beatrice for example. Premarital sex. That's probably why they did not go to church.

Pastor Freeman opened the door for Momma, Pa and I.

I strolled in before them, greeting him with a wide grin. He gave me a kiss on the forehead. I secretly laughed on the account that Pa just kissed me there when we were at home. The church basement was loud. Kids were everywhere. Massive hats, colorful dresses, and dark suits decorated the room. Shoes were shined, dresses were long and the elders were the center of attention. Maybe that's why they liked this place so much. I wondered if this is what the Jazz halls were like for adults like Nelson. Or like for Florence. Before my imagination ran off, Mrs. Burnett, waved us over. She was an elder with young features. She greeted us with so much energy.

"How are those piano lessons going," her voice was big, joyful.

I forced a smile, "Fine, Mrs. Burnett."

Gran'ma Jordan was doing most of the playing, but she did not need to know that.

Mrs. Burnett was easy to distract. A crowd of elders walked by with the energy of God and she was gone. After greeting them, I was sent off to the room full of kids where Mrs. Jenkins, a loud woman with tobacco breath, taught Sunday school for ages ten through twelve. Gran'ma Jordan taught some of the Booker T Washington high school kids on occasion for Sunday school. They would see her at the high school during the week and on Sundays. That had to be difficult.

Mrs. Jenkins set at the head of the room, like always, with her ankles crossed. Back straightened, poised. Bible in her lap. Glasses at the tip of her wide nose. Her bluish-gray dress fell past her steady bent knees. Long sleeves. Hair pinned in a low bun, the crown of her head covered with a white ruffled cloth. She and Gran'ma Jordan were great friends. They even looked alike, on occasion.

"Good Morning,"

"Morning,"

She cleared her throat.

"Good Morning, Mrs. Jenkins," I corrected.

"Forgetting your etiquette this morning, I see."

I chose not to respond to her observation and I took the closest seat near the door and waited for Ellen. John-Jon never made it to church for Sunday school.

"Bring your chair closer to the group," she eyed me. The group snickered.

I looked around. The chairs were in a semicircle. A little crooked because of me, but in its usual shape. She was still the center of attention, so what was the problem? I shifted my chair.

"Stand up, and adjust your seat,"

"Yes, Ma'am,"

The group desperately hoped for another reason to snicker during the lesson. I took the risk. Listening to Mrs. Jenkins tell the story about the creation of Eve, I raised my hand.

"Yes,"

"This question is a little off topic. Well, depending on how you look at it. It's about Jesus, so I guess it really ain't—*isn't* off topic. Well, it's off topic in relation to what you're talking about, so I—,"

"What is your question?"

"Jesus was made in God's image,"

"Yes,"

"And so were *we*?"

"Yes,"

"*We*, as in you," I pointed in her direction. "—*Me*," I pointed a thumb at my chest. "Her," Ellen was now sitting next to me. "Him," I nudged my chin in Lee Henderson's, a twelve year old who looked more like eight, direction. He looked over at Mrs. Jenkins, confused. We waited.

"Yes,"

"Why come—,"

"Why,"

"*Why* are we Black and Jesus is White? What does that make God? Why is God a man and we're not? And Eve, why didn't God speak to her? Why did he only command Adam?"

They snickered.

She smiled. Looked around, making eye contact with each of us. "How many of you have asked yourselves one of these questions,"

They hesitated. Out of fourteen of us, five raised their hand. Excluding me.

"Without looking at the exterior, the body," she brought her eyes to me. "How would you describe Jesus?"

I shrugged. She raised her chin. I cleared my throat. "I do not know, Mrs. Jenkins,"

"You have not tried, go on,"

I avoided looking at anyone. I glanced at the image of Jesus on the

50

back wall. Thick dark hair. Light skin. His eyes. Nose. Facial structure. He was white. And a man. He looked American, but I have never seen America named in the Bible. Of course.

"This will be your assignment for next Sunday," Mrs. Jenkins scanned the group. "I want each of you to think about how you would describe, to someone who is younger than you, the image of Jesus and the image of God."

Charles, a guy sitting two chairs from Mrs. Jenkins, raised his hand. "Are they the same image?"

She smiled, "You decide."

"So God created man in his own image, in the image of God created he him; male and female created he them," Ellen was getting great at quoting the Bible. "Genesis 1:27."

For some reason, in that moment, I envied her.

I did not see him come in.

The man's choir was singing today, but he was not a part of it. From behind the pulpit in the choir stands, Pa's eyes shifted from Momma to me. Momma let me sit in the back pew while she set in the second pew behind the elder women, missionaries in white. Ellen and I were still waiting on John-Jon, who we had not seen in a while, when I noticed A.C. coming down the aisle. He was wearing a hat. Tailored bottoms. White long-sleeved, collared shirt with a dark tie. Like Pa's. His overcoat was draped over his right arm. He was alone.

"He looks different,"

I ignored Ellen's whisper, but I agreed.

He was walking in my direction. Well, more like walking down the aisle to sit next to his mother, the first lady, but I would rather think about it the other way around. His eyes searched the church. Anxiety shot through my stomach. I glanced over at Ellen, dragged my eyes back to him. For the first time, I felt embarrassed watching him. I looked away. Pa was speaking with the men in the choir. I glanced back. He was closer. Close. I did not know what to do with my hands, so I placed them on my lap. Without looking down at them. Without looking away. His right eyelid lowered. He winked. His right eye winked. *At me?* He was gone. Now I could only see his back. He greeted his mother with a kiss to the cheek and a hug. She was just as happy to see him.

He winked. At me. "Did you see that?"

"See what,"

"He winked,"

"What,"

"He winked at me,"

Ellen rolled her eyes. "It didn't mean anything,"

She wouldn't understand. Her Pa was a drunk and sometimes treated her Momma like Nelson treats Beatrice. Feeling bad for my thoughts, I cleared my throat and decided not to say anything else about it. Searched the church. "Where the heck is John-Jon?"

John-Jon, his Momma and Pa managed to make it before benediction. I stopped wondering a long time ago what took them so long to make it to church. Sure, their house was further away, but that was no excuse. They lived in one of the Shanties along Archer Street. Though, his Pa had a motorcar. Some people have the privilege to still be loved by God, even when they are delayed in showing their appreciation. That was something Momma would say. There was nearly no point in coming so late. Service came to a close after a third delay from Pastor Freeman and the choir's Holy Ghost. At the end of service, we grew tired of standing around our parents while they showed off newborns and exchanged boring gossip. We met outside the church near the steps.

"Ever wonder what the Jazz halls are like?" I watched the two of them.

"No," Ellen's right foot beat John-Jon's to a ball of dirt. Kicked. It shattered. "John-Jon?"

He shook his head, jumped to another rock.

"What do you guys dream for, kicking the largest rock?"

Ellen glared.

John-Jon kept his eyes on the ground. Found another rock. Kicked. "What's going on in that head of yours," he knew.

"I want to sneak into one," I whispered the obvious as if God himself was standing in the open church doors. I took a seat on a lower step.

"Into which one," John-Jon mumbled, wiping a bead of sweat from his forehead. Though the morning was cold, it was hot in the afternoon. His eyes stayed hidden under the brim of his hat.

"Any Jazz hall,"

"That's new, bored with the usual," John-Jon raised his chin, revealing his eyes and cutting them in my direction. "Sneaking around on your Gran'ma," he laughed. "Where is she anyway?"

"She went to visit one of her friends in Muskogee," I thought about what he said. "And jumping taxis to Dreamland without actually watching a show is not exactly exciting anymore."

"Which hall you want to start with," Ellen came and set near my side, wrapping her arms around her knees.

"I don't know yet, but I can find out —,"

"What are you three out here talking about, Pumpkin Head?"

I froze. Ellen's eyes bulged. John-Jon returned his gaze to the ground. Searched. Pa glared from them to me.

"Nothing, Pa," I smiled.

He took a seat on the higher step behind Ellen and I. "Jonathan,"

John-Jon looked up, held eye contact. "Yes, Sir?"

"How about we shine those shoes today and leave the dirt on the ground?"

He smiled. "Yes, Sir,"

"Pa, where is Momma," I took the heat off of John-Jon.

"Talking with Mrs. Burnett,"

I looked away, watched John-Jon. His hands were behind his back. His eyes on the ground, hidden. I bet he wanted to kick another rock, but was too, afraid? Afraid, of Pa? There was nothing to be afraid of. He was harmless.

"Pa, did Pastor Freeman's son go to jail? Up in Chicago?" I figured asking him without Momma may result in a different response.

He cleared his throat. "Yes," it was a warning not to be too loud. Members of the church were moving closer to the doors. I whispered. "Why?" He did not seem worried to answer. "Some people were born to break the rules."

Ellen and I exchanged glances. She smiled. Pa was watching me so

I did not return it. We took that as permission to sneak into a Jazz hall.

"What do you mean," I focused on Pa.

Pa lowered himself to a step next to Ellen. Pulling off his fedora, he placed it on top of my head. It covered my eyes. Smiling, I pushed it back so I could see. He looked from Ellen to me. "If some rules were not broken, there would be no changes," Pa's eyes looked forward. He examined the road. "Change is necessary when rules begin to impose upon the freedoms of people," Pa's gaze returned to me. He was smiling.

"James," Momma's heels clapped against the concrete behind us. Paused. We looked over our shoulders. She straightened her dress, dusting invisible lent from her waist. Pa stood, walking up a few steps and extending his arm. She slipped hers into his, kept her eyes on us. "How have you two been? This daughter of mine has not invited you two over for super this weekend," Momma's neck rolled over, her chin hinting in my direction.

I hesitated, remembering her saying that I had to obey Gran'ma Jordan and not be around them much while I was under her watch. And what about Nelson? Beatrice? What was going on with them?

"I—,"

"You two are welcome to come by this evening," Momma finished.

Pa cleared his throat, but said nothing.

Momma's invitation was sealed with a smile.

Chapter Eleven
Fluid

It was perfect.

We set around the table trying to look as normal as possible, hiding the planning going on in our heads. John-Jon and I were waiting on Ellen to do her part. She was to play sick, but not too sick. Not sick enough that they would send her home. Sick enough that she would separate from us to lie down for a bit. An excuse to keep them here longer. Later.

Pa had cleaned up John-Jon's shoes real good and handed them over with that satisfied grin that set on the corner of his face. John-Jon looked down at those shining black shoes and a grin lit up his face. "Thank you, Mr. Lavelle!"

"That oughta last you a while if you avoid kicking those rocks, Son," Pa jerked his chin in John-Jon's direction. "You're becoming a man, Son. Take pride in what you have even if it does not seem like much."

"Yes, Sir,"

Pa stood and pulled on his jacket. The dark jacket complemented his pants. He looked from John-Jon to me and back at John-Jon. "I will only be a minute,"

"Yes, Sir,"

"You two hold down the fort. Check in with Ellen. I will inform her folks that she is here letting her stomach settle. She probably ate too much of your Momma's best dish," Pa was proud. Looked at John-Jon. "I will assure your parents that you are here. I'll be checking in on my shop, getting the supplies that I need and will return here. Immediately. Then, I will show you how to fix that pocket watch."

John-Jon was proud of that watch. It was given to him by his uncle who never returned from the war. Though, I had forgotten all about it. He kept it hidden in his right pocket and only pulled it out whenever he was nervous. John-Jon had done his part well and gave Pa a good reason to go to his store to grab materials to fix that broken pocket watch. Pa was thrilled, blinded by his passion of being such a helping hand.

Now, it was my turn. John-Jon waited in the living room, dangling on the courting chair Gran'ma Jordan gave to Momma months ago. Said she had no room for it in her bungalow anymore. Or use. Though, I thought maybe she asked Momma for Pa and Nelson to bring it over because of me.

I walked into my folks' room where Momma set in the sitting room to the left from the entrance. Their room was the largest in the house. Momma had decorated the sitting room with all white curtains and pillows. Pa made chairs that were soft and comfortable enough to sit in there for hours. They were white, clean. Momma did not allow much food in there. Just books. Lots and lots of books. Her sewing machine was nearby. I ran my fingers across it.

"Ma," my voice was small. She did not hear me. "Momma,"

She looked up from her Bible. She had a smile in her eyes. "Yes, Honey,"

"Ellen wants to go home,"

"Your Father will be back shortly, he can-,"

"We rarely get to spend much time together because of Gran'ma Jordan, would you mind if John-Jon and I walked her home,"

"Honey, I was not finished with what I was saying,"

"My apologies, Momma," I laid it on thick. "But, I really want to spend more time with them. She said she was not too sick to walk home,"

"Your tone,"

"Yes, Ma'am,"

She searched my eyes. "The sun has gone down," her voice was firm.

"Momma, she does not stay too far,"

"What did I say?"

"But Momma-,"

"What did I say," she did not wait on an answer and went back to reading. I looked down at the sewing machine. I thought it would be easier. Momma seemed like she had been in the perfect mood.

"Momma,"

She looked up at me.

"Do you not trust me,"

"Certainly not,"

"But Momma-,"

She raised her hand. "I do not feel comfortable with you," her left eyebrow raised. "Either of you," she glared at me. "Out so late. Supposed something were to happen?"

"Momma, Greenwood is safe. We know everybody. Besides, I'm not a baby anymore," I raised my chin. Stood taller.

She smiled. "You're still my baby and your Father's baby. You know if you ran into your Father this late, he would be torn I let you out of my sight,"

"But Momma, we won't be seen. We'll tell him you walked most of the way with us,"

She paused. Searched my eyes again. "How about I do walk with you,"

"No," I said it too quickly. "I mean,"

"What are you three up to?"

I frowned, played innocent. "What do you mean?"

"Don't forget that I am your Mother," she eyeballed me. "Now, what are you up to?"

I wondered if I could trust her. I glanced down at the Bible on her lap. Thought about Pa. "Where does Pa go sometimes whenever he's out this late,"

Her jaw clenched, but she smiled after. She relaxed, reached for the Bible. Flipped through pages. Did not look up at me whenever she spoke. "Ellen stays a few blocks away. I will time you. I want you and John-Jon back here no later than ten minutes. About five minutes there and five back."

We were fast. Real fast. Running like our lives depended upon it. "What did you say for her to let us leave," John-Jon asked through deep breaths. I laughed. "Hit a soft spot!" We were determined to check out the first Jazz hall we could see. Only, we had forgotten about one important detail. How the heck were we going to get in?

We lingered in the shadows watching the crowds of big furry coats, dresses, heels, hats, gloves, ironed trousers and shining boots.

"We did not exactly think this through,"

"Shoot, I thought the crowds would be so big that we could just slip on in without being seen,"

"They are big. Folks keep stopping and talking,"

"We would stand out," I looked down at our clothes. Our height. I felt my youth.

"Let's go back," Ellen sucked saliva through her teeth.

"We have to take you home," John-Jon reminded her.

"Let's hurry,"

"Wait,"

They saw what I saw. She was walking. No, staggering. Suddenly, I wished I had been alone. Nelson and Beatrice. Family business. Our business. My business. They would be home a few hours later. Like usual. He walked closely behind her with his hands on her waist, guiding her. Both of them stumbling over each other's feet. Laughing. Giggling. His head buried in the nape of her neck. His right hand slid down from her waist and between her legs, wrinkling her dress. His hand moved quickly. Hers covered his, moved it back to her waist. His hand lowered again while the other gripped her wrist. He stepped back, spun her and jerked her to him. It was a sloppy dance. Their bodies wobbled close until her back was pressed against one of the buildings. They were shadows now. Away from the light. Their bodies close. Real, real close.

"Let's go,"

"Why-,"

"We have to get back."

We made an about face and was on our way. John-Jon glanced over his shoulder. I pretended not to notice him. Waited. Then, I stole a glance back too.

March 13, 1921 | Sunday

It started with wind.

The trees danced outside my window like the shadows on my walls. A constant white light sliced the dark areas of the room in half. The light was coming from a motorcar parked outside somewheres. Somewhere close. I could hear the rumbling motor. I could hear them. A crowd talking against the storm. After the wind, the lightning came. Slowly, at first. It struggled to keep up, groaning far behind like me when I was too tired for Sunday school. Then, as if it were angry that it could

58

not walk through the front door, the thunder vibrated Gran'ma Jordan's house. I was surrounded in a sudden boom that brought life to the silent flashes of light. I wondered what the shotgun house was like right now on Elgin. Home. The porch would be flooded in the morning. I wondered where Nelson and Beatrice were. For a moment, I was glad to be here. Until I started feeling ashamed of being ashamed of our house. I guess life was weird like that sometimes.

I came to Gran'ma Jordan's the Sunday before Valentines. After church today, I thought I would be able to go home for good. Only, Momma and Pa insisted that I stayed longer. I surprised myself and did not complain. In the weeks that passed, I was letting precious time go by and had unfinished business anyhow.

Before the thunder drew nearer, lightning had the freedom to enter anytime it pleased. Silent. Within seconds, the rain began tapping against upstairs' massive windows. Slow. Then quicker. The talking got louder and their words were no longer mumbles.

"Hazel, you be careful with those piano lessons, you hear,"

"Oh, there's nothing to worry yourself about. This one knows better,"

"That's what you thought about Donna's gals, now they out in those Halls—,"

"Goodnight, Sister Simmons. You all make it home safely, all right?"

"—in those Halls gyrating,"

"See you at church, Sister Simmons," Gran'ma Jordan sounded closer.

"Hazel,"

"See you Sunday, Sister Simmons," a smile was in Gran'ma's voice.

The moving shadows paralyzed me to the bed. When the shadows disappeared with the light of the car, I tossed the blankets and ran as fast as I could.

"Slow down, don't you run down those stairs like that," she was calm. I caught my speed, evened my balance and took the last steps slower.

"What are you still doing up?"

"I could not sleep," something was different about her. I could not put my finger on it, but I liked it. "Was that Mrs. Simmons?"

Gran'ma Jordan turned to the large mirror in the dining room. "She and her family stopped by to say hello," she pulled at the pins in her hair. Her eyes were tired in their reflection.

"So late," I plopped down on the puffy chair that set in the corner of the living room near the wooden bookshelf. Swinging my feet, I watched her turn on her heels. Her hand pulled the last pin. Her dark hair fell to her shoulders. "You should wear your hair down sometimes, Gran'ma Jordan,"

"I like it tamed,"

"Of course,"

"Your tone,"

"Yes, Ma'am," I crossed my legs before she could remind me. I wanted to ask who made these rules. Who or what she was living for? God? I wonder if God had a personality. If so, and it was anything like hers, then heaven doesn't sound so fun. A flash of lightning flew across the kitchen, dining room and living room. Thunder surrounded the house again. I vibrated. "Yes, Sir," I mouthed to God, smiling to myself.

"Humored?"

"Ma'am?"

"You're smiling,"

"Yes, Ma'am,"

"Do share," Gran'ma Jordan walked to the kitchen. "Follow me,"

"Yes, Ma'am," I stood to my feet, walking at her pace to meet her. She was in a thin closet. It was tall, floor-to-ceiling. I peeked around her at sealed Mason jars full of fruit and juice. She pulled out an empty basket and three full jars. I watched her stroll across the room into the dining area. Placing the items on the chestnut table, she returned to the kitchen and opened a freezer that stood upright. It was much larger than the icebox we had. Her kitchen appliances looked like the ones they sell in the 'papers.

"Go ahead," she searched the inside of the freezer.

I planted my feet flat on the ground from standing on the tips of my toes, having been looking in the freezer behind her. Meeting her glare,

I smiled. "I was just thinking,"

"About," she stopped searching.

She seemed like she was in a calmer mood. "God," I thought about the homework we had before for church. We had never got back around to discussing that because we had switched Sunday School teachers. I had not done much thinking about it anyhow.

"What about Him," she was proud.

"Or *Her*," I suggested.

Her eyes narrowed, but her mouth stayed relaxed.

"I don't know," I looked down at my feet. The kitchen floor was tiled. A white tile was under my left foot, black under my right.

"You don't know or you do not want to share,"

"What were you like when you were my age," I blurted out, looking back up at her. "Did you ever wonder if God were Black or White? What if *he* was a *she*? What if—,"

"That is the end of that," her voice was sharp. She closed the door and let go of the freezer's handle. "It is late, go back to bed,"

"Ma'am,"

"Go back to bed. That father of yours has let you get away with asking too many questions you should not ask. We have an early start in the morning," she gestured towards the sitting room. "Go to bed."

I dragged my eyes away from hers. "Yes, Ma'am," turning my back to her, I headed toward the staircase. Not too eager. I suddenly wished I had left the hallway light on up there.

"Are you afraid of the storm?"

I peeked over my shoulder, embarrassed. Not enough to admit it to her. "No," I picked up my pace. "Good night, Gran'ma Jordan."

Chapter Twelve
Time

The Serpent.

The only time seeing Gran'ma lose her poise was the morning she discovered the snake resting on the porch. She even cursed it like it had never been cursed before. She had a shovel that I never saw her grab for. I stood back, watching. Paralyzed and not much help at all. The shovel stabbed the snake. Struck it a second time. Blood. Flesh. Oozing. A third for good measure. Cut in half. Into two. He was dead. She? It was dead. A weird thing happened to me. I could not pull my eyes away from it. I felt sorry for it. No, not sorry. Ashamed? I cried. For some snake. A snake most religious or terrified folks would not have much sympathy for. I thought I was the latter, and yet; I cried. I cried.

North Detroit.

Beautiful brick homes just below Standpipe Hill. It is where Negro doctors, lawyers, principals, teachers and the finest class of businessmen and women lived. Dr. Andrew C. Jackson, a handsome and thin man who wore dark suits with a straw hat, lived at 523 North Detroit. He had a Ford motorcar. Everywhere he drove, he took a three-legged pup he named Teddy. His shaggy head would be so proud hanging out that Ford when I would see them coming. The Tulsa Star owner, Mr. Andrew Jackson Smitherman, was an equally handsome man. He lived on Detroit too. To the left and downward from Gran'ma Jordan's at 519 North Detroit if my body were facing her home. Then, there was P.S. Thompson at 521. H.M. Magill after Dr. Andrew. Ellis Walker Woods. Thomas R. Gentry. C.D. Brown. R.T. Bridgewater back the other way at 507 north Detroit. Even in their wealth, folks on Detroit were not like Gran'ma Jordan. Just a street over was store owner Minnie Mae and her family. They too were more like the others and not like Gran'ma Jordan. Music and laughter danced together through open windows. Smells of breakfast, lunch and dinner tugged at my memory of Momma's chicken, potatoes and vegetables the last night I spent with Ellen and John-Jon. Gran'ma Jordan was a great cook too, so I was not missing out on much. But, listening to all the movement happening around us, I imagined sneaking out toward it all. To move with it. To watch. To listen. To live. To walk down to Deep Greenwood. As suspected, Gran'ma Jordan and her demands were not going to make that easy for me.

Black Keys.

Ignore them. That's what she said whenever I wanted to test out what sounds they would make. Starting point. That is all it was. She paid more attention to the white keys. They were cold. Cold and hard. I did not expect them to be otherwise. Black and white keys. More white than black. The black keys were like servants. The white keys owned the entire piano. I wanted to jam my fingers across all of them. A rush of sound, but Gran'ma Jordan was the one sitting down. The one in control. For once.

"There are 88 keys, 36 of which are black," Gran'ma Jordan read my mind. "How many are white?" She asked. I did the math, "Fifty-two." She nodded and went on, "This is Middle C," she paused, pressed down. It sounded like metal and then there was a vibration. There was a vibration inside the instrument. "Next, to its right, D," she paused. "E . . . F . . . G . . . A . . . B . . . and return to C," she did not look at me to see if I was keeping up. She did it again, now with both hands. "That is a scale, C Major Scale,"

Whatever it was, it didn't sound like much.

Newcomers.

There is some new kid at school who is interesting to watch. He laughed a lot. Real big like. Like he did not mind if we saw his missing tooth to the right of his mouth. Said he lost it when he was hunting down squirrels in Arkansas. Fell out a tree and his tooth went missing. Was not a baby tooth so it cannot grow back. Talked like he had been in Greenwood for years. Like he was not afraid of not knowing anybody. "Everybody's 'bout the same everywhere. Well, Black folks," he laughed while I watched. "White folks are different. Sometimes, you don't know if they like you or if they'll hang you. I know a lot of folks who were hung. You ain't never sent no hung man before?" No. Except for in the 'papers. The more he talked, I decided he was interesting enough to follow. Him and his family moved into the homes built by brothers. Closer to Archer near the hotels. Had to be the first place to live that his folks saw whenever they came into town. Greenwood was getting full of people all over. Newcomers had to take what they could get while people were building more houses, hotels, parlors and churches. Following him, all he did was kick rocks like John-Jon and laughed a little at the sky like him and God had something going that the rest of the world was not in on. I ran into Momma on her way to another meeting and it cut my spying short. She asked if I wanted to join her. I was not in the mood for politics so I declined, politely. Said I had to meet Gran'ma Jordan for lessons. I wanted to be like the new kid and newcomers with nothing on my mind. Laughing and treating Black folks and God like music.

Souls.

"[4]We have cast off on the voyage which will lead to freedom or death . . . For three centuries, we have suffered and cowered. No race ever gave passive submission to evil a longer, more piteous trial. Today we raise the terrible weapon of self-defense. When the murderer comes, he shall no longer strike us in the back. When the armed lynches gather, we too must gather armed. When the mob moves, we propose to meet it with sticks and clubs and guns."

He wrote a book about Black folks. My Momma and Pa talked about it plenty of times before. I spotted it lying around. Tried to read it, but did not understand it much back then. He was the man from Harvard who was in town. He is staying at Gurley's hotel. His name is William Edward Burghardt Du Bois. I had the same problem with his full name that I had

---

[4] Tim Madigan, *The Burning: Massacre, Destruction, and the Tulsa Race Riot of 1921* (New York: St. Martin's Griffin, 2001): 11.

with saying African Methodist Episcopal. I learned about him at school and in the 'papers. He is a popular man who help put together an organization that Momma talks about. The organization had a magazine called The Crisis. That sounded just as important as he did. It is a wonder to me that he was not staying at the Stradford hotel. Though, Gurley's hotel would not fall short of hosting one of Tulsa's Greenwood's finest guests.

Through learning about W.E.B. Du Bois, I learned that Harvard was a pretty big deal for white folks as Howard University was for us. I thought he was the first Negro to attend Harvard. Most of us stood corrected whenever Mr. Du Bois made it clear that he was not the first Negro at Harvard. Some man named Richard Theodore Greener graduated from Harvard College and was the dean of the Howard University School of Law from 1878 to 1880. The Greener fellow had spent time at both places. Howard and Harvard.

Mr. Du Bois had first attended Fisk University in Nashville, Tennessee. Like Howard, Fisk was a university for us. During his speech at the Dreamland Theatre, Mr. Du Bois said that he first experienced Jim Crow laws and lynching there while in Nashville. Said that he attended Harvard College despite them not accepting college credits from Fisk University. In time, he completed a second bachelor's degree in history from Harvard and awarded a scholarship for graduate school in sociology. I did not know much about sociology or no bachelor's degree, but it sure sounds nice. Like something I should do.

He talked of Europe too. Attending school in Europe. Who would have thought Negros from America could go to school in Europe? I thought about Pa's sister. An aunt I have still yet to meet. Wondered if she knew anything about Mr. Du Bois. He attended the University of Berlin for more schooling. Did she know anything about Berlin? I remember hearing about Berlin in the 'papers during the war. It was in Germany.

It was not until 1895 that he became the first Negro to earn a Ph.D. from

Harvard University. Whatever that was. Something else important. Something worth getting for myself.

Mr. Du Bois spoke about racial violence. A color line somewhere. Negro soldiers who were dishonorably discharged because of accusations. Trouble in Atlanta. Negro men accused of assaulting white women. Something about Abraham Lincoln and the Republican Party. Things were changing. Black folks leaving the Republican Party. Politics. Economics? He said that Tulsa was impressive because of the number of successful businesses. Owned by us.

I listened to Gran'ma Jordan and Momma talk about him. The day he spoke, Momma stayed for dinner. I did not realize it, but it is my guess he had hinted towards Garvey's movement back to Africa. Mr. Du Bois did not seem to agree with Garvey. He mentioned Elaine, Arkansas and what happened there some years ago. Trouble. Like Chicago. Something about sharecroppers hiring attorneys to investigate. Those who survived were arrested and tried for conspiracy.

Whatever that meant.

School.

Gran'ma Jordan knew how to read the sky. She knew what the time of day looked like without a clock. She knew when the sun kissed 6:00 AM. She could read whenever it was close to noon and prepared lunch promptly. She even knew what time I would make it in from school and asked me why my timing was off whenever I would make a detour on my way back to Detroit. I had to stop with the detours for threats that she would get some folks to watch me closely or would have me catch a taxi. I liked walking. I did not want to ride in no taxi. No matter how good the drivers' stories were. I wanted to see things for myself. Being told about things happening or what had already happened was nothing like actually *being there*.

Like being closer to Deep Greenwood. My stay at Gran'ma Jordan's was stretching far beyond three weeks. I still did not mind much. Though, it felt painfully long whenever boredom kicked in. I looked forward to the weekends to see more of my folks. Being separated from John-Jon and Ellen after school during the week were making Sundays awkward. The more time a part proved that John-Jon and Ellen were not that close. Without the three of us, John-Jon did not hang around much. Ellen told me that he was no longer up to jumping taxis going down to Dreamland or spying on folks anymore. I was beginning to feel sorry for Ellen, but she was not too sorry for herself. She had Delores. Delores Williamson. Her family owned a pool hall and grocer parlor. Unlike her Momma and Pa, who were known for their friendliness, Delores was always a quiet girl who started to sit in John-Jon's spot on the pew with us after he went missing on fourth Sunday in February, the twenty-seventh. We have not seen him at church since. He missed choir practices and Bible Studies on Wednesdays. In the time that John-Jon has been gone, there are three new families who used to go to church elsewhere in Tulsa and thirteen newcomers settling into Tulsa who decided to make our church their home. The new kid from Arkansas and his family went to another church closer to what Du Bois called the color line. Pastor Freeman got to brag about the new building being built on numerous occasions.

I tried to catch John-Jon at school. He was not up to eating at Donald's Bar-B-Q for lunch time in between school. We could not talk much during our school lessons. Church was the only place to really talk to each other. He should have known that. Maybe there was something wrong with his family. I had not heard anything. If there were, Ellen never mentioned it. I wanted to ask, but she spent most of her time whispering and giggling with Delores. Our trio was broken. I was replaced with a mute who suddenly found her tongue and John-Jon was out of sight. I started counting the days until school was over. I needed the summer. I needed my freedom.

Freeman's Music.

Momma said that I could come home soon, again. Something tells me there's more to why I'm with Gran'ma Jordan and not already home. I knew everything she was supposed to teach me plus more than she bargained for. Well, except for the piano. I figure Gran'ma Jordan has given up on that task. She had a lot to do without me anyhow. Whenever Gran'ma Jordan was out in Greenwood, after I would pretend to be either too homesick or exhausted to tag along, I used that time to take a walk outside on my own. Sometimes, I could hear music from a piano down the road. It was played in the mornings. Around eight. Gran'ma Jordan was usually long gone by then. Maybe it was played at night too, but I would never know. I had to be in too early. There was no sneaking out late, because she would check on me every so often with no specific time to keep up with. The music. The piano's melody did not sound like Gran'ma Jordan's. I suspected it was Miss Marie Freeman, Pastor's daughter. She seemed holy enough to be home alone to play. Away from those Jazz halls. I would slow my pace when walking by the Freeman's place. Sometimes, I could hear the music from the road. At times, it was slow. Then fast. It would stop without warning. I would keep walking down the road, too afraid to get close enough to run up and peak through a window for getting caught. I never knew when the piano would start up again. Sometimes it started up after a short pause. Other times, it never started up again. Making an about-face like a soldier, I would pretend to be on a routine and heading back to some place of importance. A big, empty bungalow. For the rest of the morning, I would dance around the house pretending to be in one of those pictures they show at the theatres. In a grand ballroom somewhere. Only, the music wasn't like Gran'ma Jordan's. It was like Marie's. Hopeful.

The Glass House.

It was a thin building in the inside with the walls a little close, but organized in such a way folks barely noticed. Thin, but you could walk to the very back and be satisfied with the furniture that fit into the space so neatly. Lights hovered upward above head with a piece of paper hanging from them evenly. Each on the right hand side. For sale. To the right, a long rectangular counter of glass. Most people walked in and was immediately greeted by Pa's music. Jazz, no surprise to anyone who knew him. The music popped, dipped, chimed and danced customers in as he spoke to them like he knew each and every one of them personally. In fact, I do not believe I have ever met anyone in Greenwood who did not know him.

Pa had this way with the people. He was so good at making and selling things that his mouth, quality of furniture, and trinkets brought white folks across the tracks. Not that white folks in Greenwood meant anything, but it sure did prove those Tulsa Tribune 'papers wrong. Greenwood was a place everybody wanted a piece of. Mr. Bradley, a tall and lanky pale man, came into the department store on a Thursday between months. Usually in the afternoon.

I asked him once, "Do you believe in war, Sir?" I was stalling and trying to make conversation while Pa was busy running his mouth with other customers. Mr. Bradley looked down at me, still high from his conversation with Pa and smiled. "What would someone your age know about war?"

I did not have time to respond. Pa finished making his rounds and stole Mr. Bradley's full attention. I asked Pa once about Mr. Bradley's life and if he knew anything personal about him. Pa told me he was a Christian man who was married with three kids. Regular businessman, like any other.

After school was over, I made it a habit to make my way to Pa's store before returning to Gran'ma Jordan to begin my lessons. Gran'ma Jordan timed me and asked about my whereabouts and had to swallow her words when Pa came strolling in the bungalow after me. Now, this was a detour I could make without much trouble. I had given up on A.C. Freeman ever showing up. The night we saw Nelson and Beatrice near the

Jazz hall was the last time I had ever seen A.C. at Vernon. Or anywhere for that matter. Though, I noticed Lawrence talking with one of Pa's customers on occasion. Mr. Bradley. I was waiting on him. It would be interesting to follow him out wherever people like him go after shopping in Greenwood.

Pa was rarely behind the counter. He had hired Troy who was a tall sixteen-year-old from the high school. He worked for Pa so that he did not have to quit school. Troy was able to go to school and then head straight to Pa's to stand behind the counter grinning and waiting on folks to finish talking. Pa offered him the position of working the counter after some of the athletes at Booker T. had left for work. Like Dick Rowland. He was one of my Pa's favorites, but Rowland ended up working across the tracks and no longer involved in sports at the school. It was a common thing to leave school for work. Pa believed Greenwood was going to change that.

Customers would come in smiling and leave laughing. Mr. Bradley was no different. This time, he came in looking at this and looking at that with another man he introduced to Pa as his brother from out of town. They were interesting to watch because it was only Pa's customers and Blue Eyes with his disciples that were about the only white folks I had ever seen up close. Well, there were those across Main Street I had seen when wandering too far, but that was at a distance. Pa showed off his handiwork of courting chairs, firm wooden tables and anything folks thought they might have needed for their homes. There was the huge chandelier in the back of the department store. I was not sure about that chandelier. It showed up one day when Pa first got the department store in the Williams Building. It would have looked out of place if Pa did not keep the place so clean. Pa was proud of that chandelier. It made the place look fancy. Mr. Bradley's brother had his eye on it. Was not before long he brought his wife from in the motorcar to take a look at it. She looked like she was on her way to church. Pa told them that it was not for sale, smiling. Proud. Mr. Bradley offered that if it were in his store, he would be able to sell it in a matter of minutes. "Folks around here probably cannot buy this off your hands." Pa was not impressed, but he laughed. The kind of laugh that he did when reading the Tulsa Tribune. Then, he looked up at the chandelier. Pride in his smile. "It is definitely worth the frenzy. Though, it ain't for sale." *Ain't.* I wished Pa would have said the right word, but Mr. Bradley, his brother and his brother's wife did not seem to notice. That was the end of it. Pa guided them elsewhere.

Mr. Bradley was there for a set of dining chairs to sell in his own shop in white Tulsa. His brother was there to help transport it. He escorted them to the counter while the wife stood near the door with her arms folded over her chest. She was pretty, but looked constipated for being so uncomfortable. The men strolled across the clean floors laughing and talking, talking and laughing some more. Like it were normal. Like they were not any different. I liked that, but Momma did not like how Pa sold to folks across the tracks when they felt it not okay to sale anything to us. Or to even allow us into white Tulsa except for work. "You do not need their money," Momma would declare politely whenever they were discussing the Glass House. There was never judgment lingering in her voice. She loved him too much for that, but sometimes he thought there was. In those moments, he would not say anything back to her. He would sit in silence. One time, he simply replied, "It's business."

Thursday Nights.

Fried chicken. Barbecue. Collard greens. If folks' noses were any good, they would smell all of that mixing in the air while hearing music oozing out of joints, barber shops, skating rinks and pool halls. Any Negro who worked and lived in the homes in white Tulsa were back for Thursday nights. They crossed back over the Frisco railroad tracks at the edge of Greenwood. Spending money, eating and having fun. They left their work as maids, mammies to white babies, chauffeurs, elevator operators, ditch diggers, landscapers or shoeshine boys on the other side. Those who lived in quarters on the south side came back to Greenwood and added to the crowded shops and businesses. Told funny stories of the things they see.

71

How crazy white folks were. You could hear everything clashing together like music.

I rested with my back against a red brick wall, smiling. The weather was perfect. The sun was swinging through trees and strolling feet. Across from me was Hotel Alexandra. It was a part of the Williams Building at 129 North Greenwood right near Pa's store. On the very end of Greenwood that ran into Archer Street was the Oklahoma Sun Newspaper at 101 N Greenwood. The Undertaker was to the left down Archer. The opposite end, Newman & Howard Restaurant at 322. There were so many places along each side of Greenwood Avenue, wrapping around down Archer from left to right. I tried to read every sign, every business. Mentally reading the memory of those too far to see. Which made me think about A.C. Freeman. There was so many places he could be. The Williams Building, Hotel Alexandra, Dr. A.J. Whitley, Dreamland, Little Fullman Café. Elliot & Hooker Clothing, Duncan & Clinton Grocers. Everybody had to eat. He was no different. Or, the Union Grocery. Abbott, H.O. Printing. No, he probably was not there. Colored Insurance Association. Attorneys Bashears & Franklin.

He sure probably needed some legal help.

Hooker Photography. That made me think about his picture in the 'paper. Smith Apartments. Newkirk, A. S. Titus Building. Home Bakery Shop. O.W. Gurley's Building was popular enough to attract the attention of someone settling back into Tulsa. Neeley & Vaden Billiards. Oquawka Cigar Store. Carter's Barbershop. A.J. Smitherman Offices. Goodwin Building. Hardy & Hardy Rooms. Dilliard's Shoe Shine Parlor. Dr. G.G. Patrick's. E.G. Howard Building. Bayer & Anderson Tailors. Dr. J.M. Key's office. Gentry Real Estate. Dr. R.T. Bridgewater's office. Dr. Wesley Jones's office. Royal Hotel. Earl Real Estate. Meeks Building. M. J. Lathan, Taxi.

He did not have a motorcar. He could definitely be in a taxi heading somewhere.

Woodard, S.Y. rooms? The Bryant Building? Economy Drugstore. Netherlands Building. Netherland, C. L. Barber. Attorney I.H. Spears's office. Hotel Gurley. Stokenberry Shoe Shines. John R. Bell Leasing Co. Dixie Theatre. Attorney E.I. Saddler's? Dr. P.I. Travis's office? Gibbons Restaurant. Johnson's Barbershop. White & Brown Restaurant? No. Funches Tailoring. Red Wing Hotel. Commodore's (Knotts) Cotton Club. Dr. Richard Walker's office. Dr. R.W. Motley's office? Partee Building. Daniel Clark Barbershop. Cain's Café. Madam C. J. Walker Beauty Parlor. No. Ferguson Drug Store. Stradford Hotel. Vernon A.M.E. Church.

No, he still has not been back to church. I wonder what that is about?

Newman & Howard Restaurant? H. Johnson Rooms? B.C. Franklin Attorney office. That made me think of her. Edith. Edith Franklin. Bayer Grocery. Hodnett Construction—

I grew bored.

I grew bored and tired. Tired and bored. There was too many places to consider. Not to mention the businesses and homes that were not on Greenwood Avenue. Like Liberty Café that was open day and night or Mr. and Mrs. Cornelius Hunter's place on north Cincinnati. I jumped up from my spot against the brick and headed back toward Detroit, excusing myself through a crowd of Booker T. kids laughing and talking. I envied their freedom. And their friendship.

On my way back, I decided to walk up Standpipe Hill. It was one of those evenings. Torches burning. Pointed hats. All gathered like it was some religious ritual. Like Pa talked about. I thought about getting close, but I knew better.

News.

I was right.

Beatrice and Nelson. They came to church Wednesday with Momma and Pa. Were no shows on Sunday. Walked in separately on Wednesday.

Separate from Momma and Pa. I listened in on Nelson talking to her when I was walking up the stairs. He was rude. Even while whispering. Rude and mean. Like he was talking to a child he did not love much. No considerations for her feelings. No worry about the tears and sadness in her eyes. She was heartbroken. Anyone listening could feel it. I could feel it. I hated it for her. I hated him for her. Yet, she did not. Or maybe she did? What could possibly keep her there with someone who clearly did not respect her? What was she missing? What was he to her? Her to him? Something else has happened. I overheard Momma talking at church. Something bad. Something I am not supposed to know much about. But I do. A little. I had to find out more. I had to watch things a little more closely. I could just ask Pa, but there was no guarantee that he would tell me everything. If he did, it would be like some riddle I would have to waste time to figure out. Momma said that I could come home closer to Mother's Day weekend. I had to finish out the school year with Gran'ma Jordan. That felt like a lifetime away.

Boys.

Ellen was changing on me. Shoot, John-Jon was too. I still have not seen him. Not at church. Not at school anymore. I missed him. I missed Ellen. Some older boy has caught her attention. Rowland, who plays ball for Booker T. Washington High School. Though, I don't think she caught his. She was younger. Girlish. Easter Sunday, at the Depot, Ellen pointed out toward him like he was a stranger while he was on his way somewhere. Looking busy. Looking satisfied. I never saw his face, but I knew who he was. Though, she was embarrassed to say his name out of fear that she would have to admit she was bitten. He was the guy who Pa liked on the team at the high school. I always wondered what happened to his real folks, but no one would know any difference. Ellen thought Damie, an elder who say she's not his biological mother, was actually his real mother too embarrassed for having a child and bringing him back to Tulsa to live with her folks without being married. No one else seemed too bothered by the details except for Ellen. Thinking about him, I wondered if John-Jon was leaving school for work like the others. Where would he work? He was young. Why so close to the end of the school year? Well, I suppose his family needed the money.

Good Samaritan.

Haskell Place, a short walking distance from Detroit. Right across the way was Main Street where white folks lived. I watched her slip into the door that stood in the front of a massive porch full of flower pots.

It was a routine. She would come out with a glass to feed the flowers. Each of them, equally. Humming. She would go back inside and stay in there for a while. I would find an opening in the back of the bungalow near the sitting room. She would be in the kitchen cooking something. Something good, I imagined. She would disappear from sight and be gone for a while. I could not see much when she disappeared upstairs. The house belonged to a woman who never came outside much after her husband died. I have seen the lady twice now. She can walk, but not well. Edith Franklin would help her, offering her support under an elbow and with an arm wrapped around her waist. Guiding her. Her hair is white and thin. Like her body. It was no wonder she had trouble walking. Edith would feed and talk to her. Though, she did not seem to say much back. Edith just kept on talking anyhow.

The Letter.

I was a liar. I was a thief and a liar. Liar and a thief. Does not matter which one comes first. I did it. I did it. I broke into that old lady's house. They think it was someone else. Someone white because she lives so close to the color line. It was not anyone white. It was me. Me, but I did not say a word. I figure, it was about time white folks get accused for something they did not do like the Black folks Mr. Du Bois talked about. But, I was wrong. I was wrong and I knew it. I still did not open my mouth.

Instead, while they talked to the Negro sherif about the broken glass to the window, I made myself comfortable in my room at Gran'ma Jordan's and read the letter that I found. Her name was on the blank side of

75

stained paper.

Edith Franklin:

You ought to know that it was a great surprise to run into you, again. You have arrived at superb timing. Next month, Dr. W.E.B. DuBois from Harvard College will be coming to Tulsa to lecture. While his visit may convey that Tulsa is moving in a forward direction, I assure you; there is a lot of work to be done. First, let me give you a proper welcome and offer you my sincerest apologies.

When I stepped off that train, I was blinded by the sun in the east. Squinting at its greeting. It was as if it knew how dazed I had been. As if that was not enough, one look around and several months since my visit felt like a century. There were more buildings and more people. The women. The women were still beautiful. You were beautiful. It was a surprise to numb eyes that had witnessed so much death to get another opportunity to see a woman so alive. A woman I had met before in passing through towns. I imposed upon you then. You, vulnerable; and I too angered by America's greed to recognize my own.

Where is your loyalty? It was a question my Father asked when the United States finally unveiled the illusion of neutrality and joined the Great War.

Every man has an internal battle to impose on anyone willing to stick around to find out. An old-fashioned man, who married a beautiful and spiritual woman, my father Ellison Aaron Freeman; a man who fit somewhere between religious tradition and a Negro politician who gave orders to his only sons from behind a desk or books. He fears God. He fears the absence of a soul in the eyes of a dead man. He fears murder, but somehow still questioned his sons' refusals to support a war. Democracy. The war for democracy is here. From Chicago, Mississippi, Detroit, Washington, Florida, Alabama, Harlem, and Texas. My piece of democracy was in the freedom of the eyes closing while the mind struggles to grasp a sense of reality at the tranquil glimpse of a woman's power. Tranquility that would make a suffering man pay for a madam's company to do without having to disclose who he truly is. You asked too many questions and I opted for her. A man who is avoiding himself cannot offer much to a woman who requires more. For this, pardon my manners.

Democracy, for America, is firing a man for trying to organize a union of damned good, underpaid, and overworked porters. I left for Chicago searching for democracy.

What I found was that the North and the South are like that of twins who were separated at birth, but met in the middle to discover they were mysteriously living the same lives. Like the South, the North treated Negroes as enemies only needed for labor. Regardless of the accusation of being incompetent or lazy, these days—like any other—our labor is necessary for America's prosperity. Consequently, for America, the war shifted European immigration and put a strain on bigotry. Without the influx of European immigrants, Negroes were and remain the answer to the American Problem. White women's labor alone was not enough during the war. Most white men were at war. Why not use the children of men and women who carried Western countries into prosperity for centuries? The French and British were already using their colonies in Africa for the war. It has come to pass that the United States made use of Negroes up North working in industries for little pay to fight overseas for the fantasy of democracy. The difference from our ancestors and today's generation – a difference our ancestors discovered even in the opposition of laws – we have the power of choice. We can choose to fight for our right to build a legacy within our communities and families—in spite of the flaws of America's so-called democracy—or we can decide to accept the conditions and limit ourselves to the expectations of a world that is too confused to recognize the value and validity of the African presence. An African presence that historically and presently occupies every land tainted by arbitrary cartography. I refused to participate in a war to be treated like useless pieces of furniture and thrown out and picked up by the French who know too well the humanity of the Negro, compliments of colonization and global enslavement. Fighting in a war, under the command of a man who would call me nigger whether I was in uniform in Europe or working the trains in Chicago, is not exactly what I would consider patriotism for an American Negro. In spite of my own reasoning, I tip my hat to those who had the courage. Your brave Father and the gift he left you come to mind. Thank you for sharing that with me. I offer my respect to him and my apology to you.

On that evening, when I approached and kissed you, I later joined my brother in his pursuits against my better judgment. Advancing without your permission requires no excuse. When Lawrence, who you now know takes full advantage of the black market, reintroduced me to you at the Depot; I suspected that you would not want to see me again. I listened carefully to your voice. Like I had remembered. Boley, Oklahoma. You stated you were here to meet an acquaintance. A stranger. Forgive me, but you are a bad liar. I knew it best to allow your attempt at discretion to go unchallenged, but I tested the boundaries and asked if this stranger was providing a room for your stay. You play a tough game. How is Florence's abode treating you? If it proves uncomfortable, I am staying on Detroit. Though it appears improper, there is an empty room available while my elder sibling, Marie, is out of town. I will take a second opportunity to honor your dignity and reside with Lawrence if you shall decide to stay.

SUMMER'S DEBT

Chapter Thirteen
Faith

"**Faith**,"

That is my name. Though, I am – Esla – at school. Faith Esla Lavelle. Faith. It was a boring name. A safe name. Momma's choice. How can someone with a name like *Faith* break any rules? If no one else, I was tied to God's judgments. I will think about all of that later before repenting. Tonight, I am breaking the rules. Again.

"Esla," I corrected.

She looked over at me like she knew what I was planning. Her smile winked from the corner of her mouth like Pa's. We were meeting for the first time. Of course, she came on the worst day. May showers and spring tornado weather. There were plenty of rain, mud and wind to cause a problem for me later when I had to do chores before heading back to Gran'ma Jordan's. We were all huddled up in the living room. Lightning flashed and thunder rolled in making Momma move around like she was cleaning. She kept pausing and looking through the white curtains she stitched up and placed near Pa's bookshelf. Pulling 'em back as if she was afraid a tornado was coming right on down the road.

"You think she'll be alright in all this, John,"

"It cain't be no better in France, Sweetheart," Pa laughed a little. He was relaxed on the sofa with a newspaper in his face. Right leg slightly crossed over the other. That's when I noticed that he was wearing his Sunday shoes. No boots. I looked back across the room. Momma was wearing her best Sunday's dress. Colorful, trimmed just above the ankles. Embroidery on the chest that made her look more delicate. Black leather heels that laced up past the ankle, hiding under the full, flowing dress.

"Who are you looking for, Momma?"

"Your Aunt Angela," she looked through the window again. In the same moment, we could hear heels smacking against the porch. Momma snatched open the door just as Aunt Angela made it. It seemed like she had been running. She was getting herself together. Her head was down for a moment, watching while she was kicking at residue of rain that wasn't going anywhere. It soaked her dark heels and black stockings. Though her legs were covered by a long beige coat with large buttons, her protected ankles hung out and I could tell she was a pretty thin woman. A little taller than Momma. Not quite as tall as Pa. Safe on the porch and aware that the door was open, she peeled off her red hat and shook it. The black feather sticking out of a dark silky ribbon stayed put. Finally, she looked up at us.

"Enchantée," her teeth were so white. There had to be more than thirty-two. Full smile. Pa's eyes. No, Gran'ma Dee's.

Momma and Pa responded to her in French. It came down to me. Big Head was gone. I could not depend on him to save me anyhow.

"Please to meet you, too," they laughed. "You three took all the good ones," they laughed again and I just rolled my eyes, smiling. Enough of that, brief introductions and she was in the house like she was not a stranger.

She spoke like everyone else for most of the time. Anything else in French I could not understand or have the patience to figure out. Though, there was one word I particularly liked and decided I would hang on to it. *Gratuit*. That is what Aunt Angela said back when Pa asked her how she felt while living in France. The word almost sounded like a sneeze. If he did not know any better, Pa might have said excuse me or repeated his question, but he seemed to know exactly what she meant. He smiled before declaring that that is exactly how he felt living in Greenwood. I wanted to ask for the word's meaning, but did not want to interrupt adults while they were talking. I especially did not want them to remember I was listening in on everything to where they felt it necessary to send me away to do something. I stayed quiet and just listened some more. Made sure not to stare too long at either of them.

She travelled alone. I noted the ring on her left hand. I wanted to ask where her husband was, but felt it not my place. At least for now while around Momma and Pa. I waited until she was alone to approach her. First, I watched her. With no hat nor rain, I got a closer look at her hair. It was short. Really short. It was shiny and looked like it had been glued to her scalp. Like she had used a lot of Vaseline. Two huge curls were glued on either side of her face hooked backwards in perfect swirls. It is a wonder to me her hair was so perfect even after getting caught in the storm. Her lips were painted nearly the same color around her eyes. It was easy to tell she was just as beautiful without all of the makeup. I looked her from head-to-toe. Her dress was different. Fancier. Her smell was different too.

"You own a silk dress," I thought about plopping down on the courting chair. I stayed put standing near the bookshelf and doves. With my parents out of the room, I felt taller. Older. Did not have to cross my legs.

She frowned a little.

"Can you dance?"

Now she was smiling. "Little one—,"

"I am older than I look,"

She hummed. It was short. Still smiling. "You have seen a lot,"

"Seen what?"

She crossed the room. Gliding and peeking over her shoulder and back at me all at the same time. "What has this lil' town shown you,"

"Little? Not so little to me,"

"You know," she placed her hands on my shoulders and straightened my short sleeves. Her eyes looked into mine. I was not uncomfortable. Not afraid. Just waited. "You remind me a lot of myself," she was humming again and dusting something off my dress that was not there. "Do you like this?"

"No," it was a quick answer. We both laughed.

"It is the proper way, here. You know, there is a whole world out there?"

"Tulsa does me just fine," I held my chin high. "You know, if you stay longer, maybe for the summer? You will see all of everything I see. The music. The food. The people. People keep on coming. The families. The fun. The—,"

"Lynching,"

I winced.

"Segregation," she stepped back. Looked off. "It is no wonder that brother of mine has taken a liking to those clubs," I waited for her to say more. Only, Momma and Pa walked in. They looked from her to me and back at her. Then me, again. She smiled, laughed a little and asked, "What's for supper?"

Tulsa's Legacy

Change is necessary when rules begin to impose upon the freedoms of people. Gratuit. I looked it up in one of Momma and Pa's books. The word means free. Well, staying home during the night was imposing upon my freedom. This was my only chance before more family was in town. Before our place and Gran'ma Jordan's would be crowded the closer to Mother's Day. Aunt Angela was staying with Momma and Pa. Most of Pa's family would stay there, though; Gran'ma Jordan's place offered more space. It all worked out in my favor. Even God did His part. The storm was over and I was able to make it back to Gran'ma Jordan's. Closer to Deep Greenwood. I could not turn around. Gran'ma Jordan would be asleep until six in the morning. It should not take me long. I will be back by then.

The streets were dark when I came. Pressure wrapped around my torso and made my legs feel heavy. In the dark, I lost track of whose bungalow was whose. My stomach was warm and jittery, but I was not thinking about no fluttering butterflies. It was a feeling like something or someone was after me. Something I could not see. I gasped and quickly looked over my shoulders. Nothing, but my eyes were wide. Searching. I tried to see as far as I possibly could. For some reason, like an idiot, I had always imagined nights to be full of light with no lingering shadows. I was wrong, of course. Walking down Detroit, I twirled in circles every so often whenever the wind picked up and blew something across the street behind me. More like jumped. Twirling was more pleasant. The silence was loud. The wind danced with the trees. The crickets provided the music. Together, it was creepy. Listening to the noises outside my window, while inside the house, was beautiful. Walking in the midst of it in the middle of the night was probably the dumbest choice I have ever made. I thought about turning around. Gran'ma Jordan's house was just a few homes down. I could turn around, run back to her house, and be safe. Safe? I am safe. It was already done. I am here. I could not turn back. Not now. My stomach tingled. I glared over both shoulders. I am already here. I cannot turn around, but something inside of me told me to run. There had been light at the end of the street. Just run. Run until I get

83

closer to the light. Run. I did. I ran. Then, I heard it. Heard it and I saw it. Light. Two headlights. One of Gran'ma's visitors? Momma and Pa? Aunt Angela? More family? It was too late. Why would any of them come this late? I stopped too soon. The gravel pulled from the ground. I lost my balance and plunged forward. My knees were warm. Blood? No, pain. Just my palms. The light drew closer. I scrambled to my feet. I did not know who lived in the house to my left because of the dark, but I ran in that direction anyway. There were bushes there. Bushes and rocks. Stones. No lights were on. No light. No way to see me. I stepped behind the stones. The bushes were like trees. Tall. Damp. Scary. Something could be hiding in them. Me. Spiders. I jumped, smacking something from my side. When fear subsided, my brain registered the familiar feeling. The leafy arm of a bush. What was I thinking? Why didn't I just go back?

The car slowed down. Whoever was inside saw me? I was caught. If it were one of the women from church visiting or anybody who could recognize me, Gran'ma Jordan will not let it get by her nor Momma or Pa. Three whippings. Three. I crouched down lower. Deeper. I could smell dirt. Dirt and spiders. Whatever they smelt like. I cringed. Prayed, stopped midway whenever I remembered I was disobeying my folks. I could not see the street. The bushes hid both the car and me. The lights. They were turning. In my direction, light stabbed through bush branches discovering me. I laid flat. The scent of dirt was stronger. The ground was cold. Damp. I did not care. I just watched. Listened and watched. Maybe it was Mrs. Simmons. If I was caught, I should just get up. Get up and pretend I was homesick. I was trying to get home. See Momma and Pa. It was a lie I could pull off. The engine shut off. The lights died. The motorcar was parked nearby. The gravel rattled under the pressure of someone. I held my breath. Whoever it was, he or she was wearing boots. The boots clapped steady over the gravel. Stopped. I held my breath. Another door opened. A second set of footsteps. Boots. Steady.

"I will carry those inside,"

It was *him*, I think. What was wrong with me? It was not him. Maybe I was already bitten by a spider. I stretched my eyelids a part. I could see the light clearly. I still had control of my body, my vision. No sign of poisoning. The ground was so cold without holding on to the near start of summer.

"Thank you,"

Edith. A.C. and Edith. Together? I had to see. I could have been wrong. I was wrong.

Whoever they were, they were walking. Separate. The sound of their boots did not match. I waited for them to talk again. I needed to hear their voices one more time, to be sure. It did not happen. The woman did not speak and neither did the man. I did, however, hear the front door of the house close somewhere behind me. Pushing myself up from the dirt, I turned around. Still crouched with the bushes, I glared up at the bungalow. It had two floors, like Gran'ma Jordan's. Several windows decorated the outside walls. A veranda wrapped around into a broad sitting area. I could not see the steps leading up to the veranda because of the dark. I knew they were there, but at night and from the angle I stood, the bungalow looked like it was floating in the air with darkness underneath it. A distant light in the living room brought color to the curtains in what I would imagine was a living room and dining room like Gran'ma's. Two shadows passed through the window on the left. Both shadows had on hats.

I was not caught. I smelt like mud, but that was not so bad. I had to find a way to see inside without being too obvious. I took a step forward. A thin branch snapped under my left boot. I kept moving. Surely, the front door was locked. I would not walk through the front door anyhow. The side of the house was covered in the same untamed bushes. I could not walk to the back of the bungalow. Like when in New Orleans with Gran'ma Dee. Or maybe I could. I wish I did not have on a dress. Overalls. That would have been perfect. There was sound coming from the far left side of the bungalow. Sound, like a window was opened. I had to risk drowning in a bush. Taking off Pa's fedora, I tucked it under limbs and leaves near the bottom of the stone gate. I felt for a rock, lowered it on top of the hat so that it would stay there whenever the wind picked up again. Pulling my piggy-tail down closer to my neck, I secured it in a ball. Tucked the leftover tail. Through the bushes, I followed the sound of voices and made sure I was light on my feet. Something thin and invisible slid across my face and I immediately knew it was a spider's web. I squatted, screamed under my breath. Shivering, I shook my dress and wiped my hands over my face and hair to be sure it was gone. Jiggled a little, kept walking. Coming to a stop underneath the window, I sucked in a deep breath and let it out slowly. Stretched my feet until I was on the tips of my toes.

I was not wrong. I listened.

"A woman should not be out alone so late," A.C. paused, gestured toward her. "In your condition,"

Edith Franklin looked cold. Cold and afraid. Not afraid, but unsure. She was wearing a dress. Silk. Gloves. The fedora. The boots and fedora were more *her*. The dress was not. It did not fit. It looked too heavy, but was perfect around her shoulders. She stood in a wide door-less entryway to a large room with a piano, chair, bookshelf and big light covered with glass on the ceiling that was all closer to the window. A.C. was calm. Turned in my direction for a second, glanced down at a pocket watch. Placed it back. He was wearing a bow tie, black shining shoes and a fitted vest where he placed the pocket watch. Its thin gold chain hung near his waist. He turned back to face her.

"It is not getting any earlier,"

"Well, that's depending on how you look at it," she giggled.

He stood on the opposite side of the room near the piano. The piano, like Gran'ma Jordan's, stood in the corner of the room at an odd angle. From my angle, Edith was in front of him, his back turned to me. Her trunks were near one of the feet of the piano. It looked like her eyes were looking right at me.

"I am free, aren't I? Or is that reserved for *free men*," her eyebrows jumped, waited.

"Lawrence has quite the imagination," he did not sound amused.

"I suppose he does," she relaxed against the frame of the entrance.

"He is the safer of the other men who keeps his company,"

She grunted, the dismissal of a warning.

"Florence is now a friend of yours?"

She frowned. "I would not exactly consider the likes of her a friend,"

86

"Likes of her," he took a seat in front of the piano. His back still to me as he was facing her in the entryway.

She cleared her throat, stood up straight. Pulled at the gloves.

"Greenwood has more to offer than the things that they do," he promised.

"You may have the wrong idea, how about I enlighten you?"

She leaned forward, tossing the gloves at him. Smiling.

"Spare the details," he picked up the stray glove closer to his left foot. Set it down on the empty space next to him. "I am not interested in the work that he does," he exhaled, shifting and turning his back to her. One leg rose as he twisted his body around and planted his foot back on the ground. He opened the piano. Black and white keys. "Nor do I expect it. I brought you here for nothing in exchange."

"Would you mind," she stepped toward a seat. She was wobbly, like Beatrice at night.

He did not say anything but stood to his feet, turned and walked in her direction. I stretched as far as I could so that I could see what he was doing for her. There were newspapers in a chair hidden in the corner of the room. He picked them up, letting them slide from his hand to the wooden floor. In the same motion, a hand came to her waist and guided her to the chair. She plopped down, smiling up at him. With her in the chair and him standing over her, I could see both of their faces. From the side. He was bent forward, close after helping her. Her right hand came to his face, ran down his jawline and lingered on his chin. As if it never happened, he straightened his back and stepped away. He walked to the piano. Calm. She leaned forward in the chair, hard. She was laughing. It wasn't a normal laugh. It was a laugh people did when they were getting ready to say something that was funny to them and not funny to the person they were going to share the inside joke with. Her left arm went limp on the arm of the chair while her right hand covered her mouth.

"You're nervous," her laugh caught in her palm. He did not deny it. She tossed her head back like John-Jon does whenever he is laughing at something he shouldn't be. The fedora rolled from her head and tumbled down the right side of the chair. Her legs were not crossed, but the dress was long and near her ankles. I watched her push her body up from the chair. She moved like she was almost too heavy to finish what she started. Somehow, she managed to cross the room without falling and met him at the piano. She stopped in front of him. He watched her. When her body jerked as if it were about to tumble down to the floor like the hat, his reflexes caught her. She laughed some more, putting her weight on him until there was no gap between the two of them. "Does my freedom frighten you," it was nearly a whisper. It was a weird question.

I wish I could see his eyes. Guess what he was thinking. See if he was still calm. What would he be afraid of anyway?

"You're drunk," his voice was relaxed. Almost disappointed.

"You have never been with a drunk woman before," she giggled. "Times are changing, haven't you heard," her arms curved around his neck.

He put a gap in between them, removed his hands from her waist and peeled her arms down. "Something tells me this isn't something you would normally do,"

"How could you be so certain," she filled the gap, returning her arms to his neck. "Hmm," she hummed. "How could you be so certain," a smile was in her words. She pushed herself higher, on the tips of her toes. "Hum?" She talked too close. "I let you kiss me the first night that we met. How could you be so sure?" Their noses, their mouths were too close. "Hum?"

First, it was like a bird discovering a worm. Then, after tasting its strange deliciousness, devoured it. The second time her lips met his, she did not pull back. Neither did he. It was nothing like Momma and Pa's. It was a kiss adults did when kids were not around. Her arms tightened 'round his neck and her body forced itself closer, but it had nowhere else to go so it just moved a lot like she had a bad itch she could not reach. When he stepped back, she moved forward. Closer. Further back. Closer. Although he was pulling away, his lips never left hers. The wooden chair in front of the piano stopped him from moving any further and he stumbled backward, falling to a spot on the wooden chair. The glove he had picked up fell to the floor. Something in my gut felt weird like I should look away, but I kept watching them. She was standing between his legs.

Once he realized the chair saved his fall, his hands came back to her waist and lingered there before he finally peeled her body away from his. She straightened to her full length, standing taller than him sitting down. She was smiling. His hands came up to hers still behind his neck. I could not hear what he said, but it was accompanied with him shaking his head. Still smiling, she pulled her arms away as she stepped back. Her right hand delayed as her fingers lingered on his neck. "Your scar, from that night," she waited. He nodded. They were separated again. The gap was much larger. "You have more control than he does."

A.C. did not respond, but I wanted to know who *he* was. I wanted to know what scar they were talking about, how it got there and what night.

She turned on her heels, watched him over her shoulder as she walked and slid back down in the chair. She leaned over its arm and picked up a newspaper. Half of its contents fell back to the floor.

"Who are you," she was still laughing, holding the paper in front of her face. "Do you even know who you are," she peeked over the left side of the paper. "*Freeman*," she laughed, dropping the newspaper and tossing her head back again. "Fools," her laughter was gone. "Slaves to your own addictions," her hand came to her stomach. She was smiling, weirdly. "I feel strange," it was nearly a whisper with a giggle in her throat.

"Perhaps, you should be careful who you criticize. It will wear off in the morning."

She giggled some more, but it was not as sincere as it had been before. She rested her head back on the chair, closing her eyes. Her eyebrows were close together. She was frowning like there was pain in her body.

He did not say anything. At least, he did not say anything with words. He turned and faced the piano. The rhythm of the music began smooth and soft. It was measured and then occasionally interrupted by a harsher sound, like an argument. Up and down. Down and back up again. It went on for a while. His expression had no emotions, but the keys pulled them from his fingers.

My feet were uncomfortable and cold. Standing flat, I bent my knees and sunk to the ground. Back against the bungalow. I wrapped my arms around my knees and listened. I had been wrong. It had not been Marie playing the music. It was him. All this time. Maybe playing was not too bad. Gran'ma Jordan has not started any piano lessons where I was the one doing the playing. Doing most of the listening did not make me want to do it. Until now.

If I ever get the chance.

Chapter Fourteen
Caught

"**H**ow long have you been here?"

My body jerked, I looked around frantically. No one was standing over me. There was just a slimy slug on my ankle. A slug. I panicked. I was not home. I was not at Gran'ma Jordan's. I was still on the ground. Wet. Cold. I jumped to my feet, wiggling and rubbing my leg. I held back a scream, closing my eyes against the sun.

"I—Please, forgive me," it was Edith.

I peeled my eyes open. The window had not been shut. I reexamined my legs for more slugs. It was gone. I relaxed. Peeking inside, I searched the room. Marie Freeman. She stood over Edith. Marie was wearing a white dress appropriate for a Sunday morning. It made Edith stand out more. Edith pushed herself up from the chair, straightened the tail of her dress. With desperation in her eyes, she extended a hand out to Marie. "I am Edith," she smiled. "Franklin. Your brother informed me that you were out of town and would be," Edith's voice trailed off. "Returning."

Marie ignored the gesture. "How much is this kind of thing,"

"Excuse me," Edith's hand lowered back to her side.

"You're no kin to the lawyer here?"

She shook her head, "No, I—,"

"I take it you are here entertaining my younger brother. I hear he spends so much time on Archer since he has returned and not in church, I figure it is only reasonable to suspect him to participate in the entertainment,"

"I am not a prostitute,"

"You are not a wife,"

Edith pulled at the silk, but kept her chin high. "I assume you are familiar with your brother's respect,"

"A man who has respect can still be attracted to a woman," to my surprise, Marie smiled. "How did you meet him?"

"Bo—the Depot. Lawrence—,"

"You are nervous. Relax, what is done is done. You have also met Lawrence," Marie's tone was loaded.

"Yes, at the Depot, but—"

"How long have you been here?"

"Not long. Only for the night, I—,"

"The night? Are these your things?"

"Yes, I—,"

"Are you planning on staying longer?"

I dropped down to the ground. Marie was walking straight in my direction towards the trunks on the floor near the piano. I was already in a heap of trouble. Getting caught now would just be embarrassing. Ellen and John-Jon would die from laughing if they ever found out. Maybe.

"You look like you could eat a decent meal. I take it these are yours? Get dressed. I should have something prepared that exceeds my brother's skill. You can thank me by joining me for church,"

"I do appreciate your invitation, but I am in search of a job and a permanent place to stay. A.C. has been quite generous, but I believe it is best if I do not make myself too comfortable. I will get dressed and be on my way. Thanks again for your invitation. Perhaps, another time,"

"Do you know what day it is?"

I did not hear Edith reply.

"It is only Friday, another time is for certain. How about this Sunday?"

"I am not sure—,"

"Believe me, you need to go to church,"

"Excuse me,"

"You tell me you are not a prostitute, but the more I look at you," I imagined Marie appearing like Gran'ma Jordan. Towering over Edith, looking down her nose. "You even smell like that poison,"

"I do not wish to disrespect you, nameless woman, but please excuse me,"

"'Nameless wom—',"

"You never offered your name, but let's not worry ourselves about that now. Please, excuse my invasion,"

I heard a commotion. Walking across the floor. I wanted to stand and peek in, but I did not want to be discovered.

"It is a shame. A disgusting shame, women like you,"

Silence. More walking.

"Who do you think you are?"

Silence. Walking.

"Women like you should be lynched."

For a moment, I heard nothing. "I'm sorry you feel that way. There's enough of that already happening." The walking continued. "God bless you."

I felt guilty. I felt guilty and stupid.

The more Momma cried, the dumber I felt. Pa was calm. He was standing in the doorway like an unwanted guest, leaning against the frame with his hands stuffed in the pockets of his trousers. He looked exhausted, but calm. The morning sun brightened his brown skin from his nose down to his Adam's apple. He stood there for a while. Quiet. In the dining room, Momma was sitting in a chair in front of me looking miserable. She had pulled the chair from its spot at the opposite end of the table and placed it right in front of mine. If we both leaned forward, our nose would probably touch. She was that close. Gran'ma Jordan stood with her chin high and her gaze glaring down in my direction. She was probably why Pa was so far from us. Either her, or he wasn't as calm about things as he appeared. I had no clue where Aunt Angela was. Could she have seen me? She seemed nosy enough.

"Where were you, Honey?"

"I just took a walk," I answered for the third time.

"'Just took a walk',"

"Yes, Ma'am,"

"Without asking for permission? What time did you leave?"

"I don't remember,"

"Watch your tone," Pa's words were measured, but he sounded so far away from way in the living room.

"Yes, Sir,"

"James," Momma glared in Pa's direction. He did not look in ours. He stayed there. Now looking out the screen door.

"Explain the condition of your clothes," his voice was steady.

"I—I fell,"

93

"How, where," Momma's questions were frantic. What was she thinking had happened?

"I don't know. I tripped over a stick in the street,"

"Where,"

"This street, I did not go far,"

"Gale and Fred stayed on this street some years ago,"

"Mother, what does that have to do—,"

"Were you at the Freemans?" Gran'ma Jordan held my stare.

"No,"

She turned her eyes on Momma. "I do not trust those boys,"

Momma frowned. "The pastor's sons?" Momma was as confused as I hoped I looked.

"Lawrence brings a lot of trouble around here. That brother of his may be following—"

"I don't see how they have anything to do with my daughter," Pa was finally annoyed. Maybe he had already been. He pushed himself up to his full length and headed toward us. His eyes remained on me.

"Of course you would not understand," Gran'ma Jordan's voice was low, but loud enough for us all to hear. Momma cut her eyes at her.

"Pumpkin Head,"

I looked at Pa. "Yes, Sir," he placed both palms on the end of the table with the missing chair and leaned forward. His eyes danced. Not for long, but for a moment. Long enough for me to see them. His dark pupils swerved, hinting toward Momma to his right. I waited. "Were you with Ellen and Jonathan?"

I was confused. I waited. His jaws clenched. That confused me more. "I—,"

He nodded, once. "Answer the question," his tone was firm.

I nodded. "Yes,"

Gran'ma cleared her throat.

"Yes, Sir," I corrected, out of habit.

Momma relaxed, exhaling. She looked so relieved.

Pa stood up straight. "Follow me."

Chapter Fifteen
Judgment Day

I imagined this was like walking with God on Judgment Day. We floated by Momma and Gran'ma Jordan who did not move or make a sound. Out of the kitchen. Through the sitting room. Finally, the front door. The sun was higher. I had to bring my hand to my forehead above my eyes. Pa did not stop on the veranda. He kept going and so did I. He slowed down when both of us were off the steps and heading for the road.

"Faith," he held out his right hand and waited.

"Yes, Pa," I slid mine into his and started walking with his pace.

"The most important thing to your mother and me is your well-being,"

"I know, Pa,"

"When you are not honest, we have to assume that we must do something to fix that,"

I waited.

"Do not forget that I know who you are," he paused, smiled down at me. "I know that you ask a lot of questions. Your mother says it is both a blessing and a curse,"

I looked down at my ruined stockings. Momma was probably upset. No, she was too scared to worry about my stockings. Guilt raised a little inside of me.

"When you get curious, when you start asking questions in that head of yours, promise me for the sake of your mother, that you will not disappear like that again,"

I looked back up at him, squinting against the sun. His eyes were serious. "Yes, Pa. I promise."

He relaxed, looking forward. I realized we were getting closer to the bungalow. The boulder fence. The bushes. The bright porch set high in the sun. It was less scary now and more like a white family's mansion.

"Now, explain the condition of your clothes,"

I pulled my eyes from the bungalow and stopped with Pa in the street. "Pa,"

His jaw clenched.

"I was hiding,"

"Show me,"

"There," I pointed at the fence of stones hidden in the overgrown bushes. "I was just listening to the music, that's all. Can we go now?" I was whispering, but we were the only ones outside, for now.

His jaw clenched again. "What did you see?"

"Nothing," it was a reflex. Too soon. "Pa, can we go now?"

His right eyebrow rose. "This will be the last time you're near this house, understood?"

I felt myself frown and forced my expression to relax. What was the problem? What did he know? I wondered if he knew as much as I did. Or if he knew more? I wanted to know. I wanted to ask, but I knew this was one of those moments when I was not supposed to ask too many questions. "Yes, Sir."

Parents are the closest thing to a relationship with God. I suppose that is why it would shorten days to disrespect them. That is not saying much for parentless children. Edith Franklin? Where was her folks? Why did she come to Tulsa, alone? The letter mentioned her Pa. He had died in the war, I reckon. Did she have a God to answer to? Or folks? What happen to people without parents around? For me, the world would not make much sense without either of mine. I would feel like I had nothing else to lose.

After judgment passed, Pa returned from God's throne and I was back to walking down to Greenwood by Pa's side like usual. I looked up at him while he smiled down on me. It wasn't before long I was watching him ease through crowds. Folks moved out of his way, said their hellos and grinned their smiles. Pa just kept on walking, tipping his hat or placing his right hand over his heart like he had seen someone for the first time. When folks talked too long, his body twisted slightly in their direction, but his feet kept moving. Our feet kept moving. They would get the point and keep it short, still smiling. Still talking. Bouncing to Pa's beat. Heck, I started smiling and talking myself.

"Where we headed, Pa? To the Glass House?"

96

"Just for a quick stop and then wherever the feeling takes us,"

"What feeling,"

"That feeling you get whenever you're doing whatever it is you do," he looked down at me, winked. I smiled and kept walking. I did not care about my ruined clothes much. He did not seem to care either considering he did not send me off to change. Until, I saw them.

Mr. Bradley's brother and his brother's wife. Mr. Bradley was not with them this time. They were waiting in front of the Glass House like they owned it. Like they had built it themselves. Like Pa was one of their workers who had come to work late. Like he deserved to be fired for not being available to them until now.

"Pardon my absence. I have been taking care of this lil' one," Pa dusted my stocking. "Had a bad fall," for the first time, I believe he was embarrassed? "How is that brother of yours, Sir? I suspect to see him this month. I have been needing to speak with him."

He ignored Pa's question. "I am here to inquire about that chandelier and a few other things I noticed upon my last visit,"

Pa loosened up. Smiled a little. "Remember, the chandelier is not for sale, Sir," his voice was still strong.

"My wife here cannot stop thinking about that fine piece of work,"

Pa strolled around Adam and Eve. They moved along with Pa. Pa stretched the door open with his left arm and gestured for me to walk in first. I hesitated. "Ladies first, Sweetheart," Pa assured me, smiling down at me with music in his eye. Sweetheart is what he usually reserved for Momma. Momma said it to me on occasion, but not often. I felt special whenever Pa said it in front of them. Like I was important, too. I relaxed, walked inside. Adam let Eve walk in after me before himself. Pa eyed the counter and I moved quickly across the floor. Troy would be here soon to take my place.

"In fact, Sir, maybe I can have the conversation with you that I was intending to have with Mr. Bradley. Since you are here, perhaps, you can relay the message."

Adam frowned. Eve crossed her arms over her bosom and eyed Pa closely. They waited.

Pa's jaw clenched. "In private, if that's alright?"

97

God and Adam disappeared deep in the back of the store. I stood looking at Eve and she stood looking at me. I decided to ask, "Where are your children, Ma'am,"

She looked around and mumbled, "Kids your age oughta be in school," she did not like talking with me. I felt it. I knew it. So, I asked something else.

"How are your children's schools, Ma'am?"

"They're just fine," she searched the place. "Wyatt, are we about finished here,"

Adam stormed down the aisle offering no words. Eve gasped whenever he snatched her wrist and charged toward the door. He paused for a moment, looking back at Pa. Pa was standing against a pole with one foot behind him. Arms crossed and cutting eyes in their direction. For a moment, he looked apologetic but his posture was too relaxed for the sympathy to last long.

"You uppity niggers. Can you believe this, Becky? Says he cannot sell anything to me,"

"It's just business, Sir," Momma would be proud of Pa.

"Who do you think you are?" He did not wait for our answer. "Business or no business, you are still a nigger."

We watched them leave.

"How do you feel when you hear that, Pumpkin Head," he came to the counter, placing both hands on the surface and shifted his weight to one leg. Waited. Suspenders, dress shirt with a collar, beige trousers. Bright, dark brown eyes. Beautiful brown skin. A trail of slight discoloration above his chest near his neck where his shirt opened. It was where he cut himself whenever he was making something for the Glass House years ago. Broad shoulders. Chin high. He needed a haircut, but he was still a good looking father. I smiled.

"You don't look like a nigger to me,"

His right eyebrow rose. "You just came out and said it, huh,"

"Sorry, Sir,"

He frowned, shook his head. "No, no, let's talk about it without silencing you and let's drop the formalities for now, alright?"

"Yes, Sir—,"

"Bumpkin Head,"

"Yes, Pa,"

"What exactly does a nigger look like—*to you*?"

I thought about Blue Eyes and Pigtail. The disciples. Ellen and John-Jon talking about slaves and Africa. About white folks. About America. About Tulsa. Greenwood. Little Africa.

"I don'know, but I don't like it when I hear it. Or say it,"

"Why not,"

"I don'know,"

"That is not an answer,"

"It is not true,"

"What's not true?"

I looked at him for a second and then looked over at the door. Thought about Adam and Eve. "What they see."

He thought about it. Smiled and did not say anything.

"Pa,"

"Yes'm,"

"Can we go inside of a pool hall?"

He stepped away from the countertop, walked around to the entry and extended a hand for me to take. "I may run into Troy on our way out." I walked with him to the door, thanked him for letting me out first and we were on our way.

We passed a lawyer's office. Shoeshine shop. Restaurant. Undertaker. Dry cleaners. Gurley's Store at 112. The Tulsa Waffle House next door. The Grocery Store, Mr. Andrew's newspaper office, the café and a Tailor across the street from Gurley's store. Bell & Little Restaurant. I pretended to be a newcomer, gazing around like I was seeing everything for the first time. On occasion, Pa let me wonder ahead, twirling around and pretending to take a photo of him with one of those nice cameras. We stopped at C.L. Netherland's barbershop near the Cigar Store that was down the way from the Billiard Parlor and Clothing Store. He must have read my mind.

"Getting a haircut, Pa," I grinned up at him.

"Yes, I saw the way you looked at my hair, Pumpkin Head. Figured it's about time if my daughter was taking a second look at it," we laughed.

We waited for a while in the shop, but that was alright for Pa. He kept the conversation going. Whenever he walked in, everybody talked at once at him like they were happy to see him. Like Helen's Beauty Shop, they talked about politics and business. Business in Greenwood and other places. Far places. There was one thing that was a bit different. They talked a lot about women. They said things I did not understand. Things that I know they purposely said riddle-like so that I could not keep up. Sometimes, their tone would be innocent, but their laughter and exchanged glares made it quite clear they were talking about things I was not supposed to know anything about. On occasion, Pa wrapped his arm around my shoulders and rocked me, asking, "You alright,"

"Yes, Sir,"

He dropped his arm and went on with the conversation, laughing through every moment of it.

Every time somebody walked in, everybody looked over to see who it was. Then, they all said their hellos and made sitting room. I was listening in on Mr. Rodney, an elder from Vernon, talk about politics while sitting in a chair getting his hair cut. That's when Rowland, the boy from the high school, walked through the door. Strolling in right behind him was A.C. Freeman.

I froze. My heartbeat accelerated enough for me to notice it and I pretended to act normal. I put my hands together and tried looking everywhere else. I thought about her. Them kissing. Not being able to look away. That's when I noticed Pa watching. I offered him a forced smile. He knew. I grew embarrassed. Pa's eyes finally stopped torturing me and looked elsewhere.

"Let's make some room," Pa tapped me with his elbow.

"Oh," I rose, feeling awkward. I hesitated. I watched the folks rise on the right side of me scoot down. I followed suit and took another seat. It was warm. The guy beside me was smiling all goofy like. I just smiled back and looked back over at Pa. Rowland took his seat near the end of the row of chairs, leaving one more available.

"A. C. Freeman, back in Magic City," Aaron Lee Donald, an elder with a big smile and tired eyes, owned A. L. Barber; the best barbershop in Greenwood they say if he talked less and worked quicker. "I just 'bout went bankrupt with you up North in Chicago. Who you let get in that head? Got your hair looking like them boys south struggling to keep the hair they got," he stepped away from Mr. Rodney who was sitting in his barber chair, the mini-afro barely touched. Mr. Rodney looked impatient, but he was still smiling.

"Looks like you got new equipment, my absence hasn't set you back too far," A.C. met him mid-shop in the four-wall shop, returned Mr. Donald's brief embrace.

"Thanks to Lawrence who comes in here about every other week, I'm getting by," Mr. Donald chuckled a little. A.C. smiled, looked around and tipped his hat to the other men. "You got a full house. Think you can fit me in by Tuesday,"

The men laughed.

"Sit on down, I'll get to you," he returned to Mr. Rodney, invading his personal space to assure him he wouldn't rush the job on account of A.C.

A.C. finally took his seat. "How's school," he looked over at Rowland. His eyes swept the room. Noticed me. I quickly looked away. Too late. "Heard you were playing basketball for Booker T?"

Rowland matures faster than his years. He never seemed to match the age of Ellen, John-Jon and I. That did not stop Ellen from growing to like him. He always seemed anxious. Always busy. Even will sitting. He fumbled with a pocket watch I usually only see older men wear. It was as if he had somewhere else to be. I never really saw him much except in passing. The long-sleeve shirt he wore was rolled up to the elbows, no collar and the tail tucked in a pair of brown slacks. His boots were unblemished.

He placed the watch back in his pocket. "Yes, Sir," he smiled. "The team is pulling together pretty good. Even after Ronnie Jefferson hurt his knee,"

"Point guard?"

"Yes, Sir,"

"How's Damie and the rest of the family?"

"Doing well,"

"Good to hear. Those grades,"

He laughed. "They weren't too bad,"

"Weren't too bad?"

"They were good. Taking some time off for work,"

"Good?"

"Very good,"

"Certain?"

"Positive,"

"Take one of R. T. Johnson's classes?"

"Yes, Sir," he shifted, looked beyond A.C. and glanced toward the glass door as folks were walking by. The sun blinded our view a little and all we could see were half of folks' bodies. Mostly their legs and feet. The rest was sunrays that made us squint if we looked too long. "Hear about any jobs," his question to A.C. came as no surprise. Due to the travel, porters were expected to be familiar with available work.

"Thought you were taking off from school for work? What you looking into now?"

"A.C., now that you back in town, aren't *you* looking for a job," Mr. Donald sounded like he was going to take matters from there and provide more information on where to find one. He did not. Instead, he stated the obvious. "I hear you lost your job up North,"

"News travel fast,"

"What you plan on doing for cash,"

"I'm taking care of that,"

"With that brother of yours," Pa joined the conversation smoothly, like he had started it.

"My apologies, Mr. Lavelle, I'm not used to you sitting so quietly. It's good to see you outside of Vernon," A.C. stood. So did Pa. They embraced like Negro men do. Warmly, but not too close. "Faith," he looked down at me from over Pa's shoulder. I waved and smiled as normally as I could.

"Good to see you too, Son," Pa's voice sounded sincere. They separated and returned to their seats.

"I hear you've taken a liken to one of those new gals from across the way," a man, getting his hair cut in the far right of the shop, blurted out.

A.C. looked the man in his eyes. "What has given you that impression," his smile was gone and he was serious all of a sudden. I looked around. Everyone else was still smiling and did not seem to catch the change in his mood.

"Few boys and I could not help but notice all the commotion yesterday evening. Surprised to see a woman like that leave with you," the man laughed. Others grunted, waited.

A.C.'s eyebrow jumped upward and lowered all at the same time. Though, his expression seemed to stay the same. "Don't let your imaginations run wild," he broke his stare and finally started smiling again, but I do not think it was genuine. He was being courteous.

"Is that a no or a yes," Mr. Lewis Berg, a barber stationed behind Mr. Donald, pressed. Mr. Berg paused from cutting his customer's hair, looking in A.C.'s direction.

"You heard the man," Pa stepped back, briefly cutting eyes at me, before grabbing the edge of the chair and taking his seat. "What she like," Mr. Berg asked.

"Can I get comfortable in my seat before the gossip starts," the men laughed. A.C. continued, "Now, tell me about how Cleaver is handling that job with those white folks as a new Negro deputy," that was all he had to say to start up on the race talk. Politics. He never answered the question. Unfortunately.

I was angry a little. Angry that adults had all the freedom to talk and ask questions. I had to just sit there and listen. Waiting. A.C. was interesting to watch alone, but not in the shop with all these men. He felt different. Older. Boring even. They should have let me do the talking, I could ask better questions and get it out of him. There was no chance.

I was ready to go to the pool hall.

It was nothing like I had imagined. No man telling jokes in the corner real witty-like. Enemies helplessly laughing. No women wearing white gloves like the ones I see Beatrice and Florence wearing. The same kind of gloves Edith had on when she was with A.C. No drunken men. Or women. Maybe it was too early. No loud music. No Jazz. But there was smoke. Lots of smoke. Away from the entrance and further back into the hall, a single light dangled from the ceiling above four pool tables. The further back in the place, the more the light looked like fog.

"Is it like this at night?"

Pa just smiled, extended a hand to the owner, Mr. Jeffrey. He would be an image of God everybody would be surprised to see. Short, with a swollen belly. He dressed nice though.

"How you doin', James, ain't sent you down here since the moon traded places with the sun,"

"Well, that wasn't nothing but early this morning if you put it like that,"

Both men laughed. I waited.

"What you got for me,"

"Them boys'll be down here close to six,"

"Six," Pa leaned the right side of his body against the counter. His elbow kept his balance.

"Yes'ir," Mr. Jeffrey lowered the front of his chest, leaning downward to fold his arms on the counter's surface. His belly hung low, but proud. "How the Mrs. feel about you getting involved in running numbers?"

Pa glanced over his left shoulder. I pretended to be busy scanning the pool hall.

"We can save that for another time. I'm here because I know you the one to come to when the 'papers haven't caught up to a good story,"

"Story, what you talkin' 'bout, just ask me and I'll tell you what I know," Mr. Jeffrey stood up straight, nearly the same height as Pa. "Now, it might cost'ja,"

"How much would I owe you if you tell me something about that girl here from Boley? Lawrence doing business with her?"

I frowned at Pa's question. Something did not feel right. His question did not feel right. What was he asking about her for? What did she have to do with anything? How much did he know about Mr. Lawrence? Why was it important for Pa to know?

"Name, Ella Franklin. Somethin' like that—,"

"Edith," I corrected, too soon to catch it.

They both looked over at me. I half smiled, pretended to look around again.

"You 'bout right. From Boley, Oklahoma. Folks from somewhere closer to Mississippi. Her father was in the war. Young and don't talk much, but smiles a lot,"

"Hmph," Pa's lips tightened. His eyebrows held on to a question he did not ask.

"She come here for reason everybody else come here. To work," Mr. Jeffrey continued.

"Work," Pa repeated.

"But she pretty, and come here alone, so that Freeman boy got to her,"

"Hmm, you know that for sure,"

"Knows it like the womens that comes here in this pool hall down to the silk dress,"

Pa cut eyes in my direction. I held his accusation.

"This daughter of mine found herself outside the bungalow out there yesterday evening,"

"Freeman's?"

"Freeman's,"

"Oh, she liable ain't sent nothing," Mr. Jeffrey shook his head. "A.C. got mo' sense. Helped her out yonder when she got ahold of that bathtub water,"

"Let her tell it," Pa never broke my gaze.

They waited. I stumbled. "I, I didn't see nothing,"

"See there,"

Pa's eyes relaxed and they were dancing again. He smiled, "Well, Jeffrey, we'll be heading out. I'll see you boys fifteen after six,"

"I'll tell'em to put their hands out!"

When we made it on the other side of the door, I did not waste any time. "Pa,"

"What's your question," he pointed to the right. I followed him.

"What's bathtub water?"

"Alcohol,"

"Alcohol,"

"Yes,"

"That's illegal, right,"

105

"Yes,"

"But, why—,"

"You ask a lot of questions, Pumpkin Head," he pulled off his fedora and slipped it over my hair. "You 'bout ready to come home,"

"No,"

He was surprised. So was I.

"Gran'ma Jordan still has not taught me much on the piano,"

"Is that right?"

"Yessir,"

"Well, learn something fast. Nelson and I have a special surprise for your Momma on Mother's Day,"

I grinned. "You gon' let me in on the secret,"

"Nah,"

"Pa, come on, I won't tell her a thing,"

"But those guilty eyes of yours will."

Chapter Sixteen
Independence St.

May 8, 1921 | Sunday

Everyone had always said that Nelson would be a carpenter and businessman when he grew up, just like Pa. It had been said so often that Nelson, without ever thinking about it, had come to believe it himself. Though, he could not build a thing that could stand distant tornado winds. Or even a blow from a child's mouth. That is why I stood shocked to see the new bungalow sitting atop that hill on Independence Street. It was proud like it knew we all were watching and waiting for it to falter; proud and smiling back at Momma on a sunny Mother's Day. Pa stood back with his fists at his sides. Nelson stood with his arms folded, right elbow in his left palm and fist under his chin like he was thinking hard about the handiwork.

Momma rushed to the covered porch, turning on her heels and slapping the air. "Now, look at this! Come on, come on! Let's take a look inside together!" Her hands and arms scooped the air telling us to come.

Grinning, I ran inside after her. Spinning around, I took in the high ceiling. There it was. The chandelier from the Glass House. Positioned high. Shining light through every angle of the dangling glass. It sent light shaped in little diamonds around the room. It was perfect. I spun and was dizzy looking at the staircase and the entrances to what I assumed were the kitchen and dining room. To the right from the front door, there was a passing area—where we were standing—that Pa called an entrance hall where a staircase was right before entering a bedroom with one bath and a small backyard porch all on the first floor. Back in the living room, passed the chimney and through a large door-less opening was the dining room. There was no entry door to the kitchen, but a door to the bedroom that led to the dining room.

"It's a little backwards, but follows the new designs," Pa explained.

Momma did not seem to care much.

From the dining room, past the small walkway and the pantry was the kitchen, an exit door to the porch with stairs and a closed entry foyer. Returning to the entrance hall, we went upstairs where there were three bedrooms with closets. Outside of the bedrooms were a narrow hallway and one bathroom. Out the window of the first bedroom was a square deck.

"Everything is about as good as new as Mt. Zion First Baptist Church they just built on Elgin." Pa sounded so proud. "There's plenty of attic space for storage," he promised. "Have the material up there to add a rail to the balcony above the porch. Safety precautions for the new addition to the family,"

"What," Nelson and I looked at each other and then at Momma and Pa. We waited.

Pa crossed the hall from the larger bedroom and wrapped his arm around Momma from behind. His eyes never stopped dancing. His hands rested on top of each other firmly on her belly. Her dress was loose. I could not tell the difference.

"What are you saying, Pa?"

"I knew it," Nelson was smiling, ignoring my question and slapping the air. "This is why you dam—dang near killed me trying to finish on time,"

Pa kissed the right side of Momma's neck and winked at Nelson and me. We laughed.

"Momma, you still cooking, right," Nelson went grinning down the stairs. "Come on now, what we waiting on? You eating for two. Let's go!"

Before I could enjoy what looked like an unlimited serving of fried chicken, mashed potatoes and peas, I was sent to the living room. The piano was delivered with the rest of the furniture. It was secured in the living room where everyone was waiting on me to prove my time with Gran'ma Jordan worthwhile. Momma was standing in the dining room entrance with a smile next to Aunt Angela. My youngest cousins from New Orleans were on the floor sneaking and hitting each other trying to be the last one to get a hit in. Scooting further and further away from each other. Faces plain and hiding laughter whenever Gran'ma Jordan would eyeball'em. Pa crunched down in front of me, telling me something about showing him what good music sounded like. Gran'ma Jordan warned me not to forget this and not to forget that. Nelson relaxed on the sofa, waiting. Beatrice had not been around for a while. I suspect she finally was free or with her own family. With uncles and aunts came a slew of cousins in town from Atlanta, Louisiana and other parts of the south I did not think to remember. All I knew is that they were all here to celebrate the good news Nelson and I had just found out. A true Mother's, Mother's Day. It was one of those months that felt full of holidays and birthdays. Nelson's birthday fell right after Mother's Day. Decoration Day was just around the corner. Most of our folks would be headed back home by Decoration Day, but still here for Nelson's. Like always. Then, there was Father's Day, except for it being in June. It would fall on the nineteenth this year. Thinking about Decoration Day and Father's Day together like that made me think about reading the letter. About Edith Franklin's father. I wondered more about how she and A.C. had met previously. The world felt small. Then, I thought about the music. The music made the world feel smaller. Closer.

I try to tell a story. I hang on to the memory of them. Playing what I had been taught, only it felt different this time. It felt real. It felt like me. Like sounds I had created myself. Before I had to think twice about it, it was all over. They cheered, clapped and laughed like I had been playing for years. I let them put on, stood and bowed. Momma shouted about how I was her precious baby. I started to scold her and Pa for making another. I let the thought pass and soaked in all of the attention before it was put on devouring the food.

"What are you reading?"

I looked up from the newspaper. "Pa, you think this will be me one day," I showed him the section with Negro graduates from Howard.

"Absolutely," he smiled, jerked his head toward the hall. "Now come on downstairs, you're missing the party. We 'bout to celebrate that hardheaded brother of yours."

"Pa, you think folks will remember me?"

"Nope,"

"What,"

He laughed.

"Pa,"

He dropped his arm from the frame of the door. "Depends,

Pumpkin Head,"

"On what,"

"On what you will do for the world,"

I thought about it.

"You have a lot of promise. You keep putting these books and 'papers lying around to use and getting in folks' business, you'll come up with some idea that'll mean something," he winked.

"Think so,"

"Certainly," he frowned, looked over his shoulder. "You smell something?"

I sniffed the air. Tossed the 'papers. "Let's go!"

Big head was twenty-three. The cake Momma made for him was huge and smelt delicious. I did not care too much for the cake, though. I knew that where there was cake, there was ice cream.

"Excuse me," the crowd did not care too much about me trying to squeeze my way through.

"Oh, Honey," Momma shooed a group of my cousins in the opposite direction. They were taller and older. Eating cake without a plate. Gran'ma Jordan was trying to get them to sit down, placing plates on the table. I kept my eye on Momma. She ducked under my cousin's long arm and reached out, grinning. "Get on out the way, come here, Honey. I have a bowl of ice cream for you!"

Chapter Seventeen
Decoration Day

"You think some kid actually fell down there before?"

"They say he died,"

"You know how parents are. They just started that lie so we wouldn't get too close,"

I listened to my cousins, squinting with my hands shielding my eyes against the burning ball in the sky. Somehow, I got dragged into Louisiana staying the night with one of Pa's sister and her husband, Bishop, who really never felt like he was married into the family. He fit right in with Pa, Aunt Eve, Aunt Angela and the rest of the Lavelles. Pa came bouncing into New Orleans like he was the President of the country returning to his hometown. So did Aunt Angela. Everybody greeted them with toothy smiles and lengthy hugs. Some folks, those who were not able to travel out to see the new house and celebrate Momma's news, were loud and screaming. I soaked it all in when they turned to Nelson and I, surprised we had gotten so big. Uncle Bishop joined the band and they were off laughing with the family and neighbors inside of the crammed, blue Creole cottage that looked like it was a house with four door entrances built right in the middle of a tiny space between the two houses beside it that would have looked the same as the other had it not been for the difference in paint.

Don't know how a house so tall and so wide could fit in such a tight space. When I peeked on the side of the blue moon cottage, there was a small wooden fence 'bout as thin as me that separated the vibrant colored homes next to it. It was taller than it was wide. I would have laughed if those houses being so close with tiny fences did not look so normal. The entire neighborhood was full of houses too close. The array of colors from the steps, walls, roofs, poles, window shutters and porches decorated the neighborhood making folks forget how close and uncomfortable the houses actually were. That was Louisiana. Just like I remembered it when I came summers ago. It was not too comfortable, but it sure was mysteriously beautiful enough to fool you into thinking that it was. Like with my cousins. I was fooled into thinking it would be a good idea to walk with them to some swamp staring down at a bunch of frog beds and what looked like a failed attempt at making an ocean's sea. It was not something you could just step into and walk clean across to land with a little water at your ankles. No, it was deep. It was dark. Dirty. Stinky and scary. Not like it looks at a distance.

At a distance, it was beautiful. It was surrounded by tall trees with tons of branches and leaves that stretched like they were waiting on music in order to dance in the water at their roots. Up close, all of that turned into what looked like a death trap. Smelt sort of like a death trap, too. The story about some kids falling in to their last breaths did not help the thought much at all. That is exactly why my body panicked and sent me screaming at the top of my lungs at Danie who was one of those cousins who lacked enough common sense to make you question your own. Pushing the small of my back, he snatched my body backwards away from the pit of hell as soon as I was losing my footing. He laughed, claiming that he had "saved my life" as if he was not the one that made me nearly lose it. That was it. I started walking as soon as I realized my feet were planted safely on the ground.

"I'm sorry about that," he was still laughing. So was his buck-toothed little brother who paused to clear his throat, slurp and spit saliva from his teeth. Disgusting. I decided not to say anything about anything and just kept on walking. "It's this way," Danie, the oldest one, grabbed my arm. I snatched it away. "Comeoncous', it was juss ajoke," I loved how his words ran together, but because I was angry I told myself he was stupid. Told him he was stupid and that he could not speak proper English. He laughed some more, "Ispeekitasgoodasya,"

I ignored him. Bucktooth started talking, but I ignored him too. They were not speaking in a language I understood anymore anyway. They laughed between words that twisted their tongues into what sounded like what English, French and Spanish would sound like if mangled together. I loved it. Was curious to ask to be taught, but not now. Not after these two tried to kill me. Second thought, maybe it would be a good idea to know what they were saying. I cut eyes in their direction. They were stepping over rocks, mud and everything else smoothly. No stumbling. Spitting. They were strolling like they knew the placement of random fallen limbs and mud puddles just fine. Bucktooth stopped behind us for a second, opened his hand for an oversized dragonfly. It flew wildly, landing in his cuffed palms. He closed his hands fast. Peeked inside. Chuckled a little and threw his arms up letting his palms free. The dragonfly flew upward, dipped. It lingered close for a second like it was now acquainted with him. He spoke to it, smiling. "Wonder if you taste as good as a mudbug."

I frowned, shaking my head. "A mudbug," I waited on an answer from either one of them. The dragonfly flew away. I would have too.

"Crawfish," Danie explained.

"Ya'll are disgusting people," maybe that's why they spit so much. They laughed. Their laugh was hearty, honest.

"Brain," Bucktooth licked his lips.

"Best part of the crawfish," Danie agreed.

"And strange people," I tripped over something hard, but I tried my best to pretend to be steady. "When is the parade?" I asked, trying to talk over my clumsiness.

"Soon, we should get back. I want to be sure to get some good throw,"

"Throw," I searched my mind to answer my own question.

"Stuff that's thrown at the parade," he spoke slowly. "Don't worry too much about the beads. Just keep your eye on the candy."

This is why I agreed to come. There was always music and candy. The good kind.

Judging the sky, it had to be about ten at night. There was no evidence of the sun having gone down anymore. Though, it was raining and I knew I was making a bad guess. That did not matter too much so long as it was dark. The rain put a damper on our return back from New Orleans, but it sure did make Gran'ma Jordan tired enough to settle in early. I slipped out the front door like I had done before. I was confident that I would not get caught this time. Even tucked a change of clothes and shoes in the box Gran'ma kept her boots in out on the porch. It was close enough to the left edge of the porch that if I needed to reach up on the tips of my toes and grab it from the ground while the house set atop a crooked hill, I could. I tossed on Pa's hat and everything was perfect. I made it down to Greenwood with no troubles. First, I waited. Then, he came out walking. I hung back some.

Folks were minding their own business for once. Then, all of a sudden, I heard him ask, "Should you be home?"

I continued walking. Crossing Archer, I cut through a crowd of men. I struggled to keep all movements natural and calm.

"Ay', should you be home," it was no longer a question.

Without looking back, I walked like I knew where I was going. A quick glance over my left shoulder, I scanned the crowd. Dim hotel lights illuminated dusty hats, boots and glass bottles. The men returned to their conversation. To the left and right of them, there were smaller groups of people standing around. Nobody walking in my direction. I relaxed. The group ahead was much larger. Men and women congested the side of the road in front of the IMPERIAL hotel. Getting closer, I immediately recognized that they were white. Women and men. Elders. For some reason, I felt surprised. Like I was seeing Santa and discovering that he was not real. Well, at least not real in the way that folks made him to be. Just a regular ol' rich Nicolas standing around in a place full of life and color. They were not much different from me. From us. Up close. Except for their skin. No, that was being nice. They were stiff-like. Almost out of place. But one. One of them looked like he was having about as good of a time as the rest of the Negro folks around. All of them were smiling, but he was grinning and bouncing. I knew better than to stare too long though and scrambled around them. I gasped at the feeling of a wet hand that enclosed around my forearm. I spun. The chest of an overweight White man collided with my face. His collared shirt damp with sweat stung my nose. My head was exposed to the warm gust of wind. Father's fedora hit the dirt. I should have left it, but I wanted it to cover my face if I needed to. I jerked myself out of his clammy palm and scanned the ground. Turning full circle, I pushed at the figures encircling me in a cocoon of fumes from alcohol. The fedora was kicked to the right, stepped on and slid further right. Back to the left, I launched downward and stretched. The gravel was warm and hard against my knees. "Negro girls have no class," a dainty voice above me mingled with the laughter of more women. A firm grip returned to my wrist and twisted me back to a broad sweaty chest.

"How much, I'll take you across the tracks to get more than the two or three dollars you negro girls make around here. Ten dollars, like the sound of that," his breath was hot and foul.

"Woodrow, she look a little too young. You hear? Besides, she wouldn't be worth that kind of money. She's just a nigg—,"

I leaped forward. The white man's grip tightened and in the same moment the ground moved.

"Where you goin' with that gal, boy?"

To my left, A. C. tipped his hat. Smiling. "Have a good evening, gentlemen," his free hand pressed against my lower back. Curls of hair fell and wrapped around my neck. With a free hand, I grabbed as much as I could, twisted and tucked. With the opposite hand, I placed the fedora back on top of my crown, holding it in place.

Furious, I glared over my shoulder. "Did you hear that?"

"Why are you out so late," his hand dropped from my lower back. I watched him search his pockets. The absence of pressure from his hand slowed my pace. Taking control of my own footing, I watched him.

"I'm looking for my brother," it could have been the truth.

He slowed down, searched. Pulled out something small. It was too dark to see. Stopping completely, he brought what he found to his mouth. Flicked it. A lighter. The flame flickered against his brown skin. He lowered his hands once the stick was lit. A cigarette hung comfortably between his lips. His right hand slipped the lighter back into his pocket. He squinted against the smoke that blew in our direction. "I saw you at the Depot. Did you follow me from there?" His pace returned to normal.

I have never been caught before. Well, at least not by the person I was spying on. I had not prepared myself to answer any questions. All I had were questions of my own. I suppose this is why I follow them. Men. Women. Children. Some of them my age. Most of them older. Elders were too religious to keep my interest. They were always headed to work, church, home and church again. Like Gran'ma Jordan. On the northeast of Tulsa, north side of the tracks, there were enough churches for anyone to attend a different church every Sunday of the year. To me, they were all the same. The difference only lies in tradition. And generation. Gran'ma Jordan said women now are losing religion. Getting bold. Whatever that meant. I refocused. There was a horrible smell coming from the cigarette.

"That stinks," I pointed, pretending to be too disturbed to answer his question.

His eyes lingered onward. A hand pulled the cigarette from his mouth and let it fall to the gravel. He stopped briefly, crushing it. Continued walking, eyes forward. "Where do you stay?"

My body was tired and my stomach was empty. I had to get home. "Independence Street," I figured it would not hurt to tell the truth. Besides, I felt proud about the house Pa and Nelson built.

He glared down at me. "Independence? You walk all the way here,"

"No," I felt like I was lying, but offered no further explanation.

"Do you still see segregation when you look around," he remembered.

I smiled; let it dissolve when he did not return it. "What are they doing on Greenwood?"

"You've gotten older, more curious about what's going on out here. You should not be out alone, this late." I said nothing, watching him. I thought about Edith. Wondered where she was. Glanced over at him. He was far more attractive than his brother. Under the shadow of his fedora, up close, he appeared mysterious. I could look at him longer without Pa around to see. I retraced his dark eyebrows. Eyes, pointed nose and mouth. He was too polished to smoke. In the 'papers, he had no hair on his chin. No hair above his lips. Up close, the short hairs made him appear older. Not older, but better. Somehow. I lowered my eyes, ashamed. Suppose this is what Gran'ma Jordan meant by bold. I kept my eyes on the ground. Rocks shifted under my weight and pressed against the sole of my boots. "You're staying with your Grandmother, on Detroit?" I looked back up at him. "You followed me from there?" I did not admit it, but I did not deny it either. "I'll take you home, have a talk with your Grandmother."

"No," maybe he saw the panic. Heard it. "I'll return on my own.

Promise I won't do it again,"

He searched my face for a second. "Go down that way. No shortcuts, no alleys through buildings. I'll be behind you at a distance making sure that you make no detours."

While I walked, I glanced over my shoulder on occasion. He was always there. I would have been afraid had I not known the shadow was him. Before going down Detroit to Gran'ma's, I called out to him. His shadow shifted. "Do you think God look more like them?"

He didn't answer.

"Hey, do you think God look more like them!"

Silence.

"Hey!" Maybe he didn't hear me.

"Could very well look more like you."

Chapter Eighteen
Lynching

"Nab Negro for Attacking a Girl in an Elevator,"
— Tribune, City Edition, May 31, 1921

"**N**ow, why'd they gon' and say that for,"

The Tulsa Tribune wrote something about Dick Rowland. Something bad.

We heard it from our friends, who got it from their friends. Who, I am guessing, flipped the story somewhere down the line before it made it to our trio. That's right, we were back. Ellen, John-Jon and I. Only, this time, we were joined by Delores and the new kid who moved to town from some small place in Arkansas. I never heard much about him since he started going to Dunbar until John-Jon brought him around. He talked real funny. Slow-like. Slower than usual, but he was smart and sort of cute if you looked at him from an angle with the sun in your eye. He was going through that awkward phase where his voice was beginning to crack. His name was Spinner. A nickname. Said his name was really Sam, but he did not like it much. Spinner could spit through his teeth like the folks in the country. That is partly how I noticed his missing tooth. A perfect line of saliva squirting to wherever he aimed on the ground. Like Pa's folks in Louisiana. He even held his body like him. Proud, comfortable. Like he owned something. For that, I didn't mind him busting up our trio. Delores on the other hand, well, her type of quiet had to grow on me. I always caught her staring real funny. Like she was afraid or something. I asked her what was wrong a few times. She assured me that she was okay. I figured whatever it was, it will come on out eventually.

The end of the story that we got was that some folks near Deep Greenwood saw the police stop Rowland in the street and put handcuffs on him. From there, he was hauled to the city jail on Second Street. According to the story Ellen got, he was not at the jail at all. She said he was at the County Courthouse on Boulder Avenue so that he won't get lynched because of the stories in the Tribune 'papers.

"You climb the roof yet," John-Jon changed the subject.

"Not yet, Pa talking about adding a rail,"

"Oh,"

"Only, he ain't started yet. He been too busy talking to Momma's stomach. Though, she ain't hardly showing,"

Ellen grunted. I watched her smile. It faded. "Why they want to lynch him anyhow?"

"Have you been listening," John-Jon shook his head like he was annoyed.

"They say he tried to assault a white girl," Delores' voice was so quiet and small.

"No, they say he accidently tripped and grabbed her when he tried to get on the elevator," Spinner corrected. He was new and was already in on how word got through to Greenwood. I smiled, a little. Wishing it were better news.

"What was he doing on an elevator with a white girl," Ellen waited.

"It's the only one we can use. Negro restrooms down at the Drexel building, my Dad say," John-Jon sounded exhausted. "He liable to be tired,"

"Tired of what,"

"All these white folks,"

"John-Jon," Ellen warned like they were around to hear.

"What,"

"You ain't never really been 'round no white folk other than Blue Eyes and his disciples 'cross the tracks," I smiled, trying to change the mood. I thought about the whites on Greenwood during the night. Thought about the white man. About A.C. "She liable to be a prostitute,"

"What," their voices became one. They all looked at me real strange. Like I was crazy. I decided not to say too much. I was more curious about John-Jon anyhow.

Ellen laughed, remembering. "Wonder what happened to them white kids we saw at the tracks,"

"Ain't nothing's changed,"

"How would you know, John-Jon," Ellen challenged.

"I just know,"

"Know how," I watched him.

"Just do,"

"How would you know when they live way across the tracks," Ellen flipped her straightened hair. I repeated her statement into a question. We waited for an answer.

Delores and Spinner just stood around like strangers, waiting for the pieces to come together without asking any questions. I felt the need to explain.

"John-Jon almost killed a white boy,"

Delores looked up, almost smiled. Spinner jumped, spun. I finally got it.

"Don't stop there!" Spinner pleaded with praying hands under his chin.

"I'm a lover, not a fighter," John-Jon kicked a rock.

"What's that supposed to mean," Ellen smacked spit between her teeth.

"What it sound like,"

Spinner's fists dropped. His shoulders hunched. "It was just getting good,"

"I saw that girl again," John-Jon's eyes lowered, boots squared another rock.

"Pigtail?"

"Who,"

"The girl with the piggy-tail," I waited. "John-Jon," he did not look at me. I called his name again.

"You hear her calling you. What happened?"

"You suspect the same could have happened to Dick Rowland?"

"John-Jon, you ain't exactly told us what happened to you yet," I pressed.

"I didn't do nothing," his eyes searched over his shoulders, calmly. "Negroes are getting lynched all over the—,"

"Way on the other sides of the country," Ellen rolled her eyes. "Let's not talk about that. Unless something happened that you's in trouble for," she searched his eyes.

"Yeah, well, I did not say nothing 'cause I did not want no trouble on account of me,"

"I thought you said you didn't do anything," I squinted at him.

"This country is crazy,"

"It's been crazy. This ain't about the country. This is about you. Now, what happened," I folded my arms, wiped sweat from the folds.

"It ain't no secret no how. Nothing I care too much about,"

"That don't answer the question," I rolled my eyes.

"She kissed me,"

"What,"

"I said. She. Kissed. Me."

Ellen and I exchanged looks. Stared at John-Jon and damn it, he was telling the truth. For some reason a feeling washed over me. I felt weird. I felt protective.

"Why," Ellen asked.

"What you mean why? Why else would you kiss somebody?"

"Well," Ellen stumbled over her questions. "What did she say? How did she do it?"

"Said she ain't never kissed a Negro before and just kissed me,"

"She likes you," for the first time, Delores did not look afraid, but— protective, too?

John-Jon shrugged. "It don't matter,"

"What you mean it don't matter," Spinner's eyes were bucked. "Did she tell anybody? Anybody see you? Where did it happen? What if you end up where that man is now?"

"Rowland," Delores's voice was small again.

"Yea, where did it happen, John-Jon," I eyed him. "And when,"

He looked ashamed for a split second. Then, he shrugged again. "A long time ago,"

"What's a long time ago," I watched him.

He was more relaxed now, looking from me to them. "Why are y'all looking at me like that?"

"Do you remember anything you just said," Ellen chuckled with her words, but she wasn't really laughing.

"I said it don't matter,"

"You know what could happen to you if an elder or one of these white folks found out,"

"They oughta know she was the one who was more curious about me than I was about her," John-Jon pulled off his hat, slapped it against his knee like getting off dust.

"What was it like," Spinner's eyes were squinting now. Curious.

"What you mean what was it like? You ain't ever kissed a girl before?"

"Not a white girl,"

"Well, it ain't no different,"

"No different," Ellen grunted.

"Wait, you kissed a girl," I was shocked, but I no longer knew why I was shocked. Now that I looked at him, standing in front of me between Ellen and Spinner, I noticed something I ain't never paid much attention to before. Delores was at a distance, to my right. Across from Spinner, her eyes occasionally watching John-Jon and avoiding him whenever he looked over in our direction. She was nervous. Quiet or just shy, because of him? He was not the same boy who was afraid to look Pa in the eye. Though he had been kicking the dirt, he did it coolly, like he controlled the world. Hands in his pockets. Clenching his jaw. Occasionally looking over at us. Relaxed. I watched him. I thought he would grow up to be funny, but maybe I was wrong.

"Who,"

I punched Spinner. I did not know him much, but I shoved him with my fist in his side anyway. Not to hurt him, just out of reflex to make him shush. He was dramatic, played hurt and started chasing me with his lips perked.

"Now you gotta kiss me, make it all better,"

I ran, laughing.

Running forward with my head turned and looking over my shoulder, laughing, screaming and breathing hard. Before I knew it, my body slammed into something firm, hard and fleshy in front of me. I went down fast.

"You, aight,"

"You're Lavelle's girl. Go on home, you hear," a tall gentleman I had seen several times before pulled me to my feet and dusted me. He could pass for white, but he was black. I never quite could remember his name. There was something in his eyes that troubled me.

"Everything okay, Sir,"

"Get on home," was all he said and kept walking. Walking towards white Tulsa.

"Did you see that," I asked Spinner, since he was closer.

"See what," he looked confused and looked back. He watched the gentleman walk away. Trousers, suspenders clinging to his shoulders and a white shirt. Of course there was nothing out of the ordinary about his clothes. I searched for Ellen and John-Jon, dusting dirt from my dress.

"His eyes," I pointed out to Spinner.

"What about'em? Were they green? Hazel? That ain't nothing. Lots of folks in Arkansa—,"

"No, no," I ran over to the rest of them. Spinner followed. "Did he seem scared to y'all?"

"*Shhh*, he can probably hear you," Ellen turned to look at him walking fast ahead.

"Yeah, something seemed strange about him," John-Jon watched him walk too. "Want to follow him," he whispered. Delores looked confused. Spinner looked excited, like usual. Ellen waited on John-Jon. I nodded my head. He smirked, "Let's go."

He led the troops.

There were a group of white men, women and children standing around outside of the courthouse. We hid behind a building adjacent from a tall white building across the way far enough where we could not make out faces too well. Delores was our lookout. I kept thinking maybe that was a bad idea because she was too quiet to be heard if she needed to warn us. I figured our luck could not be that bad and started to worry less. Watched. Listened. Spinner's head was to my right. Ellen and John-Jon's to my left. From the right angle, Spinner was more handsome to me. I thought about him chasing me and wondered what would have happened if he would have caught me. Then, it came back to me. The night I saw

A.C. and Edith Franklin. I started to feel strange thinking about it so I thought of one of the most unpleasant memories I could.

It had to have been when I had gotten in trouble for disrespecting a teacher at Dunbar. Me and my smart mouth. Folks at church tried to get a handle on it. I just had a lot of questions that Pa would probably accept about me if it was not for Momma and Gran'ma Jordan. But then, not only did I get punished at school, but Momma whipped me as soon as she heard about it. Then, when Pa made it home, he whipped me too. Waiting for him was the scariest and longest time of my life. He strolled in, took off his hat and announced the news that somehow travelled all the way through Greenwood's daily commotion - with all its tales - to get to him. He was not the one for much talking. Just told me he had heard that I disrespected a teacher, an elder and that it did not matter much what was said. No explanations. No discussions. Just an understanding that I should discern what and what not to say or ask an adult. Then it happened. Fast. Like his mother in Louisiana used to do, he used a switch on me that day. A green one. Prepared and used by Momma earlier. So, by the time he used it, it was no longer slightly moist, but tough and hard. If I was brave enough, I would have told him how silly it looked for a Negro man to be whipping his Negro child with a switch like a slave owner, but that would have gotten me in more trouble.

No, that was not the worst memory. The time I had fallen from a tree. Or the time I nearly drowned holding on to dear life to Nelson's back as he swam like a fish across a river in the country. Yes, that had to have been the worst memory. It was definitely one of the scariest moments of my life. I was only six years old then, but six is a lot of years to someone who felt they were near death. I tried to warn him that I could not breathe. Tried telling him that I did not have a chance to take a breath before he went under. He could not hear a thing. I could not hear a thing. Nothing came out of my mouth but water. All I could hear was water. All I could feel was water. Could see water. Could taste water. For all I knew, my body was consumed by water. Like I was drowning. It dawned on me and I continued to panic. I did not know when we would come up. I just tried screaming. Tried telling him I was not ready. To stop. To feel me squirming atop of him. By the grace of God, he came up just in time. Just in time for me to choke. To choke and take a deep breath. Breaths. Choking was a good sign. It meant I was still breathing and clearing my airway. Though, I was still scared. I had set there on top of the dirt with my arms encircled around my knees. Breathing. Breathing. Scared, but relieved.

"It's getting dark," Delores sounded nervous behind us.

"I'll help with the look out, not much is happening anyhow. Just mad white folks," John-Jon stepped back to join her.

I focused on the crowd. "Dang, that's a lot of white people," it was more than I had noticed when we first came.

It had to have been hundreds of white people outside of that courthouse. Equal number of women and children as there were men. There was no way I would be able to spot the gentleman I ran into. He was so light, he would blend in.

"Let us have the nigger!" Their words echoed off the stone walls.

"I have to get home," it was Delores, behind us.

"What you think they're doing," Spinner whispered, ignoring Delores.

"They trying to lynch Dick Rowland, what you think they doing," John-Jon's head popped back between Spinner's and mine's. He watched. We watched.

Three white men walked into the courthouse. Some minutes or so went by. The crowd rocked, screamed and laughed. The longer we waited, the creepier it was beginning to feel.

"You think they got him in there?"

"I don'know," I hoped not.

It was not before long the three men were walking out of the courthouse empty handed. No Dick Rowland. No noose. I did not celebrate. Something told me that was not the last of it.

"I have to go home," Delores' voice revealed that she felt it too.

"I will take you," I stepped back, grabbed her hand. To my surprise, it held tightly to mine. Almost desperately.

"I will too," John-Jon joined us.

"Me too," Ellen stood by Delores's side.

"I can't stay here alone," Spinner spun with fast eyes. "What if something happens?"

"Look," John-Jon split the gap between Spinner and me and peeked closer.

We followed suit.

A group of Negro men were coming from the North, from the direction across the Frisco tracks. The first familiar posture I noticed was the owner of the Stratford hotel. Mr. Smitherman. What was Mr. Ray doing there? I thought he did not believe in war, but he was one of the men carrying a rifle. I had not seen him since Momma's speech. Things were changing. They noticed. The White folks. Some of them pointed in their direction. They looked from Sixth and Boulder. The vehicles approached and a cold silence swept over the white crowd. The Negro men were heavily armed. Guns. Fearless protection in their presence. There was a car with a shotgun riding on the side. Mr. Ray's taxi. There were plenty others. Mr. Warren. Sanders. Morgan. Mr. Jeffrey from the pool hall. All businessmen turned soldiers. Several veterans looking confident and unbothered. A lot of them, but not enough. They could easily get lost in the swelling crowd of whites who slowly noticed them coming. More whites, but not enough guns. Maybe.

"Get those niggers out of here!" This time, it was a man. The white crowd seemed to be moving away from the Negro crowd or the guns.

Willard M. McCullough, the new sheriff, came out with one of the two Negro deputies, Cleaver. I thought about what Pa said. McCullough told everyone to go home. Promised that everything and everyone—Dick Rowland—would be protected and safe. The Negros declared they wanted to be assured that the presence of the lynch mob would not result in a murder like the 'papers had promised. "If you cannot protect him, we will."

"No one is getting lynched here tonight,"

With that, Cleaver did most of the talking. He promised that Rowland was being protected, but I was not so sure. I peeked over at Spinner; the frown on his face told me he was not so sure either. Cleaver said something that sounded a lot like trouble. Like politics. About behaving. Our place. I don't know what turned them around, but they did not leave without promising to return if they needed to. They took their time leaving.

Reluctant, Mr. Ray and his troops eventually made an about face, loaded back into their cars and headed across the tracks. A few smaller groups of armed Negroes came and went. Went and came. Sometimes, they came with the same folks, checking to see if anything had started up. They were holding the Sheriff to his word and promised to hold up their end if the Sheriff had any trouble protecting Rowland. McCullough assured them and they were gone again. Though, they left the white folks shouting. Not so much about Rowland anymore, but angered by the audacity of all *niggers*. The audacity to try to intimidate them. To tell them what to do. Who they could not bring justice upon. There was talk of an uprising of Negroes. Shouted declarations that Negroes—*we*—were organizing in Tulsa and in other cities. Some of them were shouting at the Sheriff. Shouting that we needed to be taught a brutal lesson. To stay in our place. *Uppity Negroes*. Though, they used the word niggers. There was talk about our land in Tulsa. Like we did not deserve it. Others were shouting north towards Greenwood. Little Africa. I spotted a little boy with overalls. He was smiling weird and crazed. His face twisted up squinting against the sun. Sandy brown hair stretching out of a brown deformed hat. With one hand in his pocket, he raised the right one. Pointed north with his index finger. Thumb pointing toward the sky. I read his lips: *BANG*. His thumb lowered slowly and he jerked his index finger upward in the same motion like he had shot a gun before.

Delores gasped.

"They're upset," Ellen reported, whispering.

"Shhh," I listened.

McCullough tried to ask the whites to disperse. They did not. Instead, they started hooting and hollering. "The armory," one yelled.

"What's that," Delores whispered.

"I don'kn—,"

"Guns," John-Jon breathed.

"Guns," I looked over at him. His eyes were straining forward. There was a group of whites suddenly running east toward Sixth Street. Lots of them. The other portion of the crowd stayed at the courthouse.

"You think they're going to get guns?"

Ellen's question went unanswered. We did not know what was happening.

"What do you think they're doing," Ellen tried again like John-Jon was the expert.

"What else do you think they're doing after seeing all those Negroes with guns?" I searched John-Jon's eyes after he spoke. His shoulders shrugged while we were still on our stomachs on the ground. "Have to be,"

"We should go," Delores was afraid.

"We have to wait," Spinner shook his head.

It was not before long we saw some of the white folks coming back down Sixth Street, some of them empty handed and others with rifles. Some of them scattered somewhere else, away from the courthouse. Disappeared. Came back with weapons.

"We should go—,"

"Shh," it was John-Jon, Ellen and I who shushed her. Delores did not say another word.

This time, it was more Army veterans. Though, they just looked like clean and wealthy Negro businessmen. Which, judging by their sudden moment of silence, was a hard sight to see for envious white spectators. Most of them were in cars.

The noise started up again. I searched their faces. Squinted. Spotted new faces this time. Including Nelson, A.C. and Pa.

I started to run out, Spinner caught my waist. His eyes were serious like I had never seen them before. His childish, bubbly spirit had been replaced with a feeling I had only felt with Pa. Then, it hit me.

The day had started normally. Right now, people were in churches and in movie theatres. Kids, like me, were getting ready for tests to wrap up the school year and finally start the summer. Most of them were home. Where we should have been. Older kids, from Booker T Washington, were probably thinking about what and what not to wear. Getting ready to wear their finest dresses and suits to the prom. Normal lives. Normal? Not knowing what was going on outside the courthouse. What time was it? I looked up toward the sky. It was dark, but I could see movement. Clouds against a forgotten sunset.

"Let's wait," Spinner's voice was a whisper to my ears.

I relaxed. His arm released me. Glancing at the others, they weren't paying us much attention. Ellen, John-Jon and Delores were looking ahead at the commotion.

"What if—,"

Spinner shook his head again. "Let's just wait,"

"Look! Look!"

I looked, fast. My body jerked forward, I was pulled to the ground. The Negro men were returning to their cars or walking away like organized soldiers. A white man. Seemingly old, tired. He went after a large Negro man. I could not make out his face or figure in the night.

"That's Mann," John-Jon whispered.

"The veteran," I strained my eyes to be sure. My chest pressed against the ground hard and the five of us laid breathing loud and waiting.

Something was said and that was the end of it. One simple tug at the pistol and somehow it went off. More shots rang out. It was nothing like watching the kid in the overalls. Where there was no sound coming from his mouth, there was a loud sound of power with the pistol. Real. Explosive. Not distant or in my mind, but right there. Right in our faces. Our ears. The panic shot through my body and my heart raced, but I could not move. Folks just stood there watching for a moment too. Surprised. Looking down at a body just lying there. Lying there. I did not know who it was. All I knew for sure is that he was Black. Black and just lying there. They all just stood there and looked at him. Sirens. As if the crowd remembered why they were gathered, everyone went wild. Bodies of men, women and children. All running in different directions all at the same time. I still could not move. Three to four ambulances arrived out of nowhere. The crowd turned them away. They just turned off their engines and stood there too. The man was left lying in the street under a billboard of Mary Pickford's pale, American face. She was a woman I had seen before by the theatre. No one was bothered by the body anymore. The crowd devoured it. He was out of sight. Lost at the bottom of the chaos. I was being pulled from the ground, but I could not stop watching. Pa. Nelson. A.C. I searched. "Where are they?"

"Come on!"

Ellen and Spinner. I struggled to get loose.

"Let's go, let's go!"

"I can't go right now!"

"Faith, don't be stupid!"

Chapter Nineteen

Barricade

They pulled and tugged me passed the Convention Hall.

Folks were cleaning up after what looked like a pageant for white students. They were dressed pretty nice. Years ago, I remember hearing about Holy Fam Catholic School having graduation pageants at the Tulsa Convention Hall. Even the remnants of it was beautiful. I was caught staring and jerked forward. We looped around hiding wherever we could when slipping by Tulsa Central's High School on Sixth and Cincinnati. There was decorations there that read JUNIOR-SENIOR POW WOW. We kept going. My eyes were open wide. I saw an amusement rides and games. Mountain of sandwiches. Even in the midst of running and everything, my stomach wanted one. Of course, on a good day, that would not even be an option. We went along Cincinnati, heading north. We dipped behind trees. Buildings. Motorcars. Kept low. Lower. Taller. Fast. Low again. Somehow, slipping back into Little Africa, passing houses and hiding from motorcars. In Little Africa, we went block to block to block to block. From the aching in the soles of my feet and the sweat under my armpits, Little Africa was not all that small. We huffed and puffed, sucking in air walking up hills and dips in the roads and finally coming down toward Deep Greenwood the opposite way facing white Tulsa down the way like we had never been in that direction. Like we had not come from that direction at all.

Relaxing, I watched Bill Williams, the son of Mr. John and Mrs. Loula Williams who were the family who own the Dreamland Theatre. Bill was walking into the Stratford Hotel with a big smile on his face. He had no idea what just happened. His classmates were with him. Clueless. They were much older than us. Juniors at the high school. I knew what they were doing with all that colored paper. They were getting ready to hang it in the luxurious ballroom from the ceiling for the junior and senior prom tomorrow. I thought about the Catholic School and Tulsa's Central High School in white Tulsa. Looking up at the Stradford Hotel, I smiled a little. Proud. They went on about their business normally and did not notice us. They were not concerned or did not even seem to pay much mind to the growing crowd of Negro men discussing what was happening at the courthouse. We knew what to look for and knew immediately why they were huddled up. More was happening. Though, we could no longer see or hear it, we felt it.

"I'm tired," Spinner spoke first, finally out of breath. He had been running and slipping into places so fast on the way back with no trouble. It sort of surprised me to see him slumped over with his hands on his knees. I looked around. Greenwood was packed with people. I spotted pockets of men with bottles. Cursing. We jumped and our bodies followed the loud sound of a gun. A crowd of folks laughed.

"Hold on to your bullets. You might need them later,"

"Nah, there won't be no trouble here in Greenwood, boys," all I could see was the back of a head in a hat as the man looked up at the pistol in his hand. Some folks in the crowd laughed while others shook their heads. Even with the gun, their mood was light.

"What do you think is happening out by the courthouse now?"

I did not bother to answer Spinner's question and started footing it toward Detroit.

"Where are you going?"

"Gran'ma Jordan's, I'll catch up with ya'll later,"

"Esla,"

"Just going to check on her," I was walking before I finished talking. They did not ask any more questions. I kept going.

Before making the right to Detroit, I turned left and made my way up Standpipe Hill. I saw it immediately. Standing all right there in the night. A cross. Burning.

I ran as fast as I could and did not stop until I made it to the Williams Dreamland Theatre where there were crowds of people standing around outside. I calmed myself and decided not to panic anybody. I looked over my shoulder at the Dixie Theatre diagonally behind me to the right, further down. More crowds. There was a lot of commotion near the buildings on both sides of the road. A lot of movement. A lot of people. They did not seem too concerned to see me out, which was unusual. No hellos or questions about where I am supposed to be. Some folks looked around as if they were expecting to see Gran'ma Jordan or Momma and Pa. Though, they did not say anything and went on about their way.

It felt like a Thursday night, though it was only Tuesday. I looked back at Dreamland. I stood there in front of Mr. and Mrs. Williams's building with its red brick. A two-story building. An American flag proudly waved with the wind at the very top of the roofing that was mostly flat except for where the flag was and an identical rising of the roof to its left with no flag. Taking a good look at everything, I stood there reading WILLIAMS DREAMLAND THEATRE across the first floor. There was this large piece of what looked like concrete that decorated the first half like a hat. It protected people if there were ever rain. Ball lights ran along its length. Then, above the bright concrete hat, were five windows that really looked like eight. Lights on the second floor in a set of windows that had the words "Dreamland" written in lights. They popped out at anybody who was coming or going. To my left, when facing the set of entrance doors to the right, was a wooden board holding a picture of an actress I had never seen before. Long dress down to stocking covered ankles. Large hat. She was walking right off the board if you looked at it too quickly. Live musicals, bands, theatrical revues, touring vaudeville acts and silent films for fifteen cents a movie ticket. I did not have no movie ticket, but I had a real good reason to get into that theatre. I would expect a lot of folks to be inside. A lot of folks dreaming and not knowing what was going on outside of those walls. Eight hundred seats. Two shows a night. I dashed for it.

The only folks I discovered was a high school instructor and kids preparing for their graduation. I walked over to the nearest person, a senior.

"There is something going on at the courthouse,"

"What,"

"A man was shot. I don't suspect the trouble will come here, but,"

"Shot?"

"It does not look too good,"

"Shot?"

"Yes, shot. He was just lying there,"

"Young lady," the instructor walked our way. "What are you talking about?"

"There's some trouble over that boy Dick Rowland. White folks are trying to lynch him. Some of 'em stormed the courthouse. Though, a lot of Negro veterans-,"

"Stormed the courthouse?"

"No-,"

"Lynching, ol' hell,"

"I knew this would happen,"

"Gurley talked about this in front of his hotel. It will all blow over," the instructor pointed at some things sitting in a chair. "Grab your things, everybody. I would rather you be home until this whole thing is put to rest."

Some of them sighed. Others moved toward their things.

"Cannot wait until this is all over," I watched one of the seniors lean against a wall, annoyed.

Folks were grabbing their things and talking at once. I looked back over at the senior and I wanted to share more of what I saw.

"It was a Negro man who was shot and killed," my eyes searched the ground. They were all talking and moving. I heard them. "I don't think it's over," I warned, but they were no longer listening.

I had a dream once. It was strangely pleasant. A dream full of all the food and candy I had ever wanted. I celebrated, hands full and smiling – ready. Ready to devour everything my eyes laid on. Pure happiness. Though, in that same moment, I felt that something was off. Like something was too good to be true. It was not before long I woke up and discovered that the food and candy was gone. To make matters worse, it never existed. I looked around the quilt. Searched and did not find a thing. Not even an empty wrapper. It was just a dream. A dream. Then, I felt empty. No, more like robbed. Like I had had everything in my hands for it to be stripped away in only a matter of minutes. Or hours. However long the dream took to finish.

That feeling was the exact look in Momma's eyes before she met Pa finally coming into the door. We had been waiting all night. Listening, talking and waiting. Eventually, Momma kept herself busy cleaning rooms that were already clean and then finally resting her body reading the 'papers Pa left in the sitting room downstairs. Her body was resting, but her mind was not. Her thought were all in her eyes. When she looked up at me from the 'papers to ask for me to get ahold of some water for her, she had even tried to smile a little. I knew that she was as worried as I was. We could hear the occasional gunfire at a distance, but they were close enough to make Momma worry. I was mostly afraid because of what I knew. What I saw. When I thought about the Negro man lying dead in the street with the crowd watching him, I felt guilty for thanking God it was not Pa. Hoping and praying that it would never be Pa. He did not make it until midnight. Though, he came in smiling. He looked over at me by the staircase.

"Why aren't you in bed?"

"We were waiting for you," for some reason, my worry turned into anger.

"Nelson went down to the courthouse and has not been back. I thought he was with you," Momma's voice held a question that I wanted to ask. We waited.

"Relax," Pa's smile widen. "-the both of you. It's been a long day," he shook his head. Shook and stretched his arms out of his suit jacket. "Let's get some rest. They will tire themselves out. Nothing won't make me miss out on ending the day with my family in this fine house," Pa strolled over to Momma, grinning. His arms wrapped around her waist. She hesitated, eyed him closely, but rose her arms to rest around his shoulders. Hands behind his neck. "Nelson has finally snapped out of it and found something to fight for and I support him in that decision so long as he keeps an eye on your Mother. He sent me on my way and insisted I be here," Pa started rambling. "I couldn't agree more than to not worry about white folks and their threats. Their threats and lies about who we are and what we deserve. I should be able to choose to lie my head down comfortably and rest peacefully in our house. New house. In our community. Our city. Our country—"

There was gunfire and shouting outside somewhere. Somewhere close. I heard it and they did too. It was not like before. Like Thursday nights when folks were showing off and shooting into the sky. No, this was different. This sent something through Pa's body and made him look over his shoulder at the door so suddenly that I expected someone to come on through it. Momma was looking too, her chest rising and falling with an exhale. The echoes grew louder. Closer. Then a whistle. A whistle. Another. More gunfire. One shot after another. As quick as boiling water. Then, a solid shot. In the distance. Not too close, but close enough to scare me.

"Let's get some rest,"

"John—,"

Pa released Momma and strolled in my direction, scooping me up on his way up the staircase.

"I'm scared," I whispered in his ear while watching Momma stand at the foot of the stairs getting smaller and smaller. I tried to look brave and not let the words I whispered to Pa show in my eyes.

"There is nothing to be afraid of, Pumpkin Head," Pa sung with a smile in his voice. He kept his voice low.

Momma did not blink. She watched us disappear upstairs. For the first time, she did not seem too sure about Pa's tune. On the second floor, we turned and was in my bedroom. He lowered his back and I slid down from his embrace. Straightening and adjusting my gown, I looked up at him. "Will they come here, Pa?"

"Who," he pulled my quilt back and patted the bed.

"The white people. I heard Gurley at his hotel," I lied.

Pa's eyes searched mine. "How'd you get away from your Grandmother?"

We both smiled. He laughed a little. His smile shifted to the left side of his face like he knew something I did not want him to know. Then, he broke his stare and patted the bed again. I eased where he patted. Relaxed, a little. "Get some rest. There's some boys—*men*—out there who were in the war. They can handle them quite well. Maybe scare them off."

War? War. What would we need for soldiers in Greenwood? In Tulsa? In Oklahoma? In America? In our own country? This was no war. Wars happened oceans away in other places. In Europe. In places described in the Bible. Not here. At least, not the kind that required soldiers. I wanted to ask more questions. I wanted to tell Pa what I saw.

"Pa," I slipped into the bed under the quilt that he held up in one hand for me. "I—," I thought about all the white folks who were at the courthouse earlier, but I could not tell him that. That I had snuck into white Tulsa and seen what I saw. Hundreds of whites outside of the courthouse waiting to get their hands on Rowland. Men, women and children. All of them angry. If we needed soldiers, I don't think it was much about Rowland at all anymore.

"Faith," Pa looked down at me with raised eyebrows. I searched his gaze to see if he was sure. If there were any doubt. What I found was pride. Pride. In his eyes and in his closed smile. I wanted to be proud too. I wanted to feel just like Pa. So, I returned his smile and trusted him.

And the soldiers.

Chapter Twenty
Invasion

I smelt food and my body followed. When I made it downstairs, it was like any other morning with Momma and Pa. Bright and shining day with Jazz and Religion. Momma moved around the kitchen with grace, humming and making breakfast. Pa stood up from the sitting room and joined her. He added some salt to eggs against her will. Momma eyed him with a laugh in her smile. He pecked her lips and promised her he would give up adding salt whenever his heart decided for him. Momma threatened to get the salt out of the house. He laughed. They laughed. Standing in front of her three-corned stove with something different in each pot, I smiled and relaxed too. I sniffed the air, closing my eyes. Biscuits in the oven. I opened my eyes and suddenly noticed it. Propped up like it was normal to be there. A rifle against the kitchen counter by the sink. As if reality was kicking back in, I heard the hail outside that had nothing to do with a storm. Distant gunfire. No matter how long we had been sleeping.

"Get in here and eat and don't forget to say grace,"

"You won't be going to school today,"

"What about report cards?" I had never been so eager about them. I had always done excellent in my studies, but this time I was not eager to see my grades. I was eager for things to remain normal. At least school. School was always there when things seemed to change. When I had to stay with Gran'ma Jordan, school remained the same. Except for Spinner and other new kids coming, but even that was normal. And church. School and church. Moving to Independence Street. Church and school. Both the same. Some things changed, like friendships and people, but it was still the same. All getting back to normal with a little time. Today, the first of June, was the day we were scheduled to get our report cards before the start of the summer. Those long, fun summers. By the time school starts again, I will be ready to finally go to Booker T. Washington High School. I needed my report card and I needed my summer. I had unfinished business. I needed to go to school.

"I want to see—,"

"Do you hear that," Momma cut me off, but for a good reason. We listened.

"Gunfire, sound like it's coming from Archer Street and Boston Ave or First and Archer. That's where the men are along Frisco Railroad. Sent me on my way for you, Esla and the baby,"

"Gran'ma Jordan?"

"Nelson should be here any minute now with her. Forgot to mention with all the commotion last night that it was his goal to get her here by this morning. She will take some convincing. As you well know how hard-headed she is,"

"John," Momma's eyes pleaded with him.

"She insisted on staying. Said she was not gon' let no white folks run her out her own house. I had her promise that if Nelson felt like it was getting too bad that she would allow him to bring her on around this way. Plus, she had Mabel out there with her. Taking care of her like her family should—"

Mabel?

"John," Momma's voice was calm. "My Mother has her ways and so do others, but there ain't no need in talking about anybody. Including Mabel's folks. You just never know what's going on in other folks' houses. Besides, that new girl in town has been taking good care of her. It's no wonder she might be kin," her eyes cut in his direction. His jaw clenched. "I am relieved Dr. Jackson got ahold of Nelson's mind," her voice was lower that time, but firm. "You know as well as I know that you cannot choose what happens to family. It is none of our business judging folks, John."

Pa cleared his throat again, waved me over. "Stop being nosy and bring your butt over here and grab some breakfast."

I laughed, doing as I was told. I sat next to Pa. He opened the Tulsa Tribune. The Tulsa Star was already read and sitting on the table in front of him. That's when I noticed the other gun. There was a pistol on the table beneath the 'papers. Momma served us as if she did not see a thing. She was usually so cautious about things like that. Pa was never able to bring any weapons in the house. Not even the huge knives he would use after he and Nelson had gone fishing. Glancing back over at the gun and

139

over at Momma humming, I noticed the lump in her apron. The shape of the back end of a pistol. I did not know what to think of the two of them.

BAM! BAM! BAM! BAM! It was knocking, but it was too frantic to make sense to me in my head. In the same moment that the banging started, Pa was up with the pistol going for the front door. Before I realized it, I was standing up against Momma. She was holding me and I was holding her. We waited.

Pa stepped close to the window near the door, to the right. Momma had sheer curtains over those windows. I did not notice how thin they were until now. I cursed under my breath and prayed that Pa was not spotted. What would happen to him if he was spotted? What if he was not the only one with a gun? They had had plenty of guns – both Negro and white folk down by the courthouse. More whites than Negros. I didn't even know Pa had a pistol. Let alone the shotgun near the counter. Why didn't he grab the shotgun? That pistol could be too small to scare anybody away. I wanted to grab it and give it to him, but my body wouldn't move and Momma was not letting me go. Her arms were wrapped around the tops of my shoulders and around my chest. I held on to her arms and sunk in close to her.

"It's me! It's me! They're hauling out all the men!"

"Nelson!"

Pa let him in and Beatrice strolled in behind him. Both bugged-eyed. Momma told me to rush upstairs to get dressed. On my way there, I heard her asking about Gran'ma Jordan. I slowed down my pace to listen from the living room as they disappeared in the kitchen. Nelson called Gran'ma Jordan stubborn. When he started telling Momma and Pa about seeing a body in the street, Pa came around the dining room and cut his eyes at me. "Do what your Momma told you,"

"Yes, Sir."

When I made it back down, everybody was sitting at the table. Except Pa. He came back in wet, but I do not think it was from sweating. He had a bucket in his hand. He tossed it before joining us at the table. It was empty.

"Pa, why are your clothes wet,"

He smiled a little with his mouth on the corner of his mouth. "Oh, well, your Momma put me to work. Putting water on the house,"

"The house – why," I joined them in the dining room. Momma and Pa were to my right. Beatrice and Nelson to my left sitting across from one another. Nelson's eyes were drained. Beatrice set quietly, glancing over at Nelson occasionally like she was wanting to ask him something. We were sitting at the big wooden table in the dining room. There was much more room in this dining room than there were in the house on Elgin. I started searching for places we could hide if we needed to. Beatrice and Nelson no longer looked out of place sitting there. Everybody's silence was awkward and it was clear that they had been talking about some things I was not supposed to hear. Maybe I came down too soon. Maybe Pa said too much.

"Let's eat!" Momma rose and headed to the kitchen, rubbing her hands together like she was hungry. Now that she was eating for two, I imagined that all the commotion worked up an appetite for her. A whistle blew. It was close. Like a sheriff. It blew before Momma made it to the kitchen. She froze. Then, there was knocking.

No, not knocking. Banging.

"Under the table,"

"Momma—,"

"Now."

From where I was, I watched Pa grab the shotgun and hand Nelson the pistol. I rushed under the table. Sloppy and unsure if I would be good at hiding. They disappeared somewhere. I searched for their legs. For their feet. Stretched. Searched some more. The back door opened a little. Closed. Then a closet somewhere. I heard walking above. Like in the ceiling. The attic. They were not saying a word. Strangely, Momma was checking the biscuits in the oven.

When the mob came in, I heard the crackling of fire on pine knots burning. I thought about the water Momma had Pa put on the house. To protect it from burning. It was worth a try, but what happens if they got inside of the house with that fire? I looked around at all the dry wood. The cushion on the seats. The feet of the curtains over the windows. Momma's touch that made a house a home. Someone stood by the

141

curtains. Too close, I guessed. The others were walking through the house. They were grabbing things. Not just anything. One went upstairs and came down with jewelry. I saw a necklace and other pieces fall to the ground. Masculine hands scooped them back up. I scooted deeper under the table when I nearly saw the guy's face. Something else fell. A necklace, near his boot. He bent over and snatched it from the floor. I heard someone strike the piano. The piano. There was no way they could get that out. The front door was open now. I could see things happening out there through the gap. Fast moving clouds that were not normal. They made part of the sky look like night was coming, though; it was early morning. I stayed in the nook of the table. Beatrice was setting in front of me where I could see her stocking covered legs and black heels. I could not hear or see any signs of Nelson and Pa. Momma was strangely calm.

"We are eating no matter the circumstance," Momma was still cooking. They commented on the food in the pots and I heard metal clinging. Banging. The back door leading to the backyard opened. I saw the sky. Big, gray and black balls of smoke blocked the sun. Below the sky, someone from the mob threw Momma's pots in the backyard. I heard Momma whimper in the kitchen. Someone got ahold of her biscuits in the oven. Tossed them to someone closer to the back door. The biscuits hit the ground. A boot smashed them in the mud. Her beautiful, golden biscuits. I felt ashamed. Ashamed and angry that I could not stop myself from crying.

"Come from under the table, nigger,"

Momma met me and wrapped her arms around me.

I scanned them. They did not look as mean and dirty as I imagined. They wore hats, ties, collared shirts, dark trousers and shining black and brown shoes. Some of them even wore jackets over their trousers. Suits. The women wore nice dresses. There were kids there too. Looking around the house throwing things that were not supposed to be used for play. Though their clothes were nice, their eyes were not. They were smiling, but their eyes made their smiles feel cold. Like they had no soul. I looked away. Down. Momma lifted my chin with a flick of her hand, resting the back of my head to her chest. I looked forward, held in my tears.

"You got anything worth keeping," it was not a question he was waiting for Momma to answer. She was not saying anything anyway. He was gone by the time he had finished saying it. He and about six others walked toward the staircase. Some of them moved like they were shopping in a shop, grabbing things that looked and were valuable. Even pausing to gaze at their find, smiling. One lingered behind, eyeballing Beatrice. "Oh, I see something worth keeping," he grinned. Laughed a little. He stomped over to her. They all moved so quickly. As he was making his way to Beatrice, some white folks came through the door and looked over at us standing near the dining room table. Then, at Beatrice who was still sitting like she was waiting on permission to move. "There's a piano up here!" I watched the growing crowd downstairs with us. Their guns and fireballs at the end of sticks moved with them. Most of them saw the house occupied by other whites and shouted, "Go to the next one!" Crowds of whites came and left. The first mob was here to stay, leaving the door wide open for us to be exposed. They had come in their dusty cars. Some, boldly walking with bare feet. Protected by police.

Where was Pa and Nelson?

The sound of flesh hitting flesh came through the words, "Nigger, do you hear me,"

By the time I realized what had happened, Beatrice's head had turned and she was catching her fall from the chair, holding each side tightly. Her eyes were closed tight and she was crying. I wanted to do something, but Momma held on to me tightly. Momma said something. Not to me. To them. She said it again, but this time, I realized she was talking to Nelson. He had appeared in the back door holding the pistol to his side.

I have no idea why him and Pa left or what the plan was or if they had even figured out a plan. Maybe while I was upstairs changing? All I knew, whatever the plan was, if there was even a plan – Nelson was no longer playing along. Something clicked and the great fire had been lit in his eyes. To see another man lay a hand on Beatrice. I wanted to stop him, knowing his temper. But something inside of me wanted him to do something. "What are you going to do, boy," the guy laughed. Momma moved and moved again, but she was stopping herself. "Honey," her voice was pleading. She spoke to Nelson softly. He seemed to listen from a place deep inside of himself. Some place where revenge settled in. His eyes were cold. His jaw clenched and a tear rolled down his right cheek. Something told me it was more happening in his mind than what Momma was saying. More than about that man hitting Beatrice. Maybe he finally was seeing himself in that white man. Seeing what kind of man he had been to her. Having never protected her, from himself.

"Nelson, calm down," Momma spoke to his anger. I watched another tear fall from his eye. I felt it. Shame washed over his face. He wanted to protect her. To defend her. To use the strength he once used against her.

"Go," Nelson spoke through clenched teeth.

"Honey,"

"Who do you think you are, nig—"

Nelson was fully in the house. Had already pointed the gun.

There was a loud bang that vibrated everything. I vibrated. So did Momma. A warning shot. I spotted Nelson walking through the dining room pointing the rifle. He was saying something. The mobs ran toward the stairs, but they were not scared. They were laughing. They were actually laughing. They had more weapons.

"NELSON," I tried to call him back to reality.

Momma pulled my wrist and grabbed Beatrice with her free hand. We ran for the back door.

"Where you think you're going niggers. Your boy here tries to scare us and you think we're going to let you go that easy,"

I froze. The barrel of a gun was pointed in our direction. Closer to Momma.

"Go," Nelson eyed the mob, keeping the rifle pointed and steady. Where was Pa?

"Momma," my voice was so low.

The man behind the gun was grinning.

A warm feeling washed over me. It rushed through my body and in my soul. I suddenly felt my heart beating like I had been running for miles. Then, I remembered. I remembered, but I did not think about it much. It just happened. The gun was out of Momma's apron and I was holding it. I aimed. Closed my eyes. Pulled my finger toward me.

The blood. The oozing. The attempts at breathing. Surprised, shell-shocked eyes searched around the place. Mine. My ears were ringing. Somehow, I had hit my chest. I only knew because it was sore. I was on the kitchen floor. All at the same time, the floor moved. They were running. I was being hauled out. Low.

Gunfire motivated me to carry my own weight. I was up and running without having to prepare for it. Momma. Beatrice. No Nelson. No Pa. Tripping over everything and anything we could not see, yet we kept our footing. We just kept our heads up and our eyes open straight ahead. My eyelids stretched trying not to miss anything. I looked down on occasion and over my shoulders. Hoping to see Nelson, somehow. Or Pa. I was glad Momma had told me to change. I could not imagine running in my gown. Too bad I forgot to put on my shoes. We passed plenty of families in the streets without shoes. A lot of them wearing last night's pajamas. The Robinsons. The Hamptons. Tolberts. I wondered where Pa was. We did not stop until we were covered by trees, but Momma did not want to go too far. She wanted to see the house. We crouched down concerned about our family. About the folks running. About Greenwood. We had to wait it out for Nelson and Pa's sake.

Chapter Twenty-One
Summer's War

More gun shots.

War. There was a dull rumbling in the sky. I could only hear it. Balls of smoke lit up like lightning above our heads. Aeroplanes. Flashes of lights. Then, flames. Lots and lots of flames. More big, black rumbling balls of smoke. I could taste it. I thought about that dream I had. About waking up and having nothing. That feeling returned to Momma's eyes. I could see it in the light as she watched Greenwood burn. There was a heavy feeling in my chest. Guilt. For not keeping up with Nelson and Pa. For not telling enough people. For doing what I did. I did not have to do it. Maybe they would have let us go? II thought about the dead man in the street near the courthouse. Then, I remembered. Rowland. I wished I had told more people. Maybe Dreamland was not enough. I felt disappointed. In myself. For running and leaving Nelson. I tried. What else could I have done? I did not want to see what would have happened. But, what else could I have done? Momma must have felt the same. She was no longer concerned about staying low. She just stood there on her knees watching. I called out to her.

"Your Pa promised he would be here," her voice was faint. "Him and Nelson, he promised," Momma was not present. She was thinking. "What is wrong with me, what were we thinking? As if they were going to just come and go without causing trouble. Just seeing women makes things worse. They have no sympathy. No hearts. My God," she wiped her face. "What have I done? I should have let him stay. I should have listened,"

I thought about the gun. The blood. "Momma, will I go to hell?"

She cleared her throat. When she looked at me, her eyes were stronger. "You see that American flag," her voice was calm. The night was loud. It was day, early morning. But, it felt like night with the sky being so dark. It was still night, for Greenwood. For me. For us.

"Look at me,"

"Yes'm,"

"You see that American flag,"

I did. I saw it. In the distance, on Standpipe Hill. Over my shoulder where she was looking. It made me think about the preamble to the Constitution. I thought about us. Them. The people. Little Africa? Blue Eyes and his disciples. I looked around at everything and nothing at all at the same time. I thought about how proud A.C. had been. The letter. How proud folks were just hours ago. How proud Pa and Nelson were when they showed Momma the new house. The pride Pa had last night when he told me about the soldiers. The Constitution.

There was movement everywhere, but it was calm near Momma in the trees. Beatrice said nothing. I said nothing and just watched the flag blow in the hot wind.

"That means your country is at war with you," she was certain.

"Momma,"

"I cannot run for you and I do not want you to follow me. I will slow you down,"

"Momma,"

"Do you hear me?"

"Momma, I can't leave you,"

She did not say anything for a moment. Maybe she was thinking about it. I thought about Pa and Nelson. The other men. Wondered what happened at the courthouse after we ran. "What about Pa—,"

"I want you two to head towards the tracks. I heard someone mention the Midland Valley tracks on the way to north. East to Kansas City,"

"Momma, it is not safe,"

"Avoid the crowds. Negroes too, but head north,"

"Momma—,"

"Do you understand—"

Gunfire exploded over head. My body went into shock. I remember reaching. Reaching for Momma. Reaching for Beatrice. Screaming for them. Being told to shush. Being told to run. I wanted to stay with them. Why did we have to split up? That did not matter much now at all. Maybe it was because I did what I did. Maybe Momma did not want me anymore. "Go!" "But, Momma!" I wanted them to keep up. I wanted to show them my hiding spots. I wanted them to know. To be safe. Pa. Nelson. Momma. Beatrice. Gran'ma Jordan. Spinner. Rowland. John-Jon. Ellen—A.C. Freeman? Edith? What was happening to everyone? Were they running, too? I could not see faces. I could hear them. Screaming. Grabbing. Guiding. Falling.

A shoebox. "Grab the baby!" A Mother. A Father. A warning. "Don't let this slow us down," the Mother passed the shoebox to the Father. "We cannot leave the baby," he nodded, agreeing with her and grabbed the shoebox. Held it close. Tight. Too tight? Running. Running towards the tracks. He tripped. Nearly dropped it. She grabbed the shoebox, quickly. "This will not stop us! We have to bury our stillborn in the morning," she was frantic. He was apologetic. Helpless even. "Baby, we have to—," more gunfire. He ducked. She ducked and scrambled for a safe place on the ground. He snatched her up. The shoebox was gone. Out of her hands and left on the ground. "No, wait!" She reached for it. Screamed for it. I watched from over my shoulder, passing them. Gunshots. The blood. The oozing. Nelson. I closed my eyes and cleared my head. Turning, I dived for it. The mother was still screaming.

Me. I was falling, but I was getting up quickly. Too quickly. Too visible. No longer in the trees. The shoebox. The baby. The parents. Crying Mother and ashamed Father. High pitched screaming like the world was ending. A Mother's desperate yellowing that did not care about what was going on. Loud. Heavy. Uncontrolled. Full of fear and death. I did not care about being caught. I had to get the baby.

When my right foot hit the ground, I heard it. I felt it. At the same time. My lower back. The worst pain I had ever known. Not like scraping a knee, but indescribable. Pain that cannot be fixed. I wanted to reach for it and cover it, but my hands caught the ground. More pain. In my knee, the left one. The dirt smelt like summer. Like the Fourth of July, but it wasn't Independence Day. Was it? What day is it? It had to be July. The pain. July. The heat. June? The choking. May? Yes, May. It didn't feel like May. The parade. I remember. Memorial Day. May.

May? No, June.

"The railroad tracks! Go to the tracks!" It was a distant warning.

My body was heavy and my feet were bare. My legs ran beneath me, but I wasn't going anywhere. The ground was warm. There was shooting. Somewhere close. Shouting. My legs kept running. I couldn't feel my heart, but I was breathing. Yes, I was still breathing. The black smoke rising from the ground tasted bitter in my throat and burned. I was choking, but I had to keep going. If I had not heard the gunshots and the screaming, I would have stopped to catch my breath. To feel my heart. To look, one last time.

As quickly as possible, I glanced over my right shoulder. I could not recognize them, but there were people there. Small crowds fled past the shadows. Illuminated by the light. Fires. I was far behind. Too far. Closer to the gunshots. Maybe too close, but I could make it. Had to make it. If I went faster, it was possible. When my right foot hit the ground, I heard it. I felt it. At the same time. My lower back. The worst pain I had ever known.

I looked up at the sky and watched it. It was all I could do. It was still morning, passed or closer to 6:00 or 7:00 AM. No later. I could not remember. I knew two things when I opened my eyes. The first, I was alive. Pulling myself up on my elbows, I scanned the area for the voices that I could hear. Second, I was not dreaming. I stayed closer to the ground. I remembered. Searched for the shoebox. Nothing. For a moment, I wept. I could not do much else for a while. I could still hear her. The Mother. Screaming and crying. I thought about my own. Wished I could run, but I knew it was there. I did not want to look at it. I did not want to see how bad it could be, but I felt it. I did not want to see the blood. Did not want to know if I was dying. I searched the world. Trees. Sky, smoke. Ground. Screaming. Shots. War.

He was standing atop the white house. Right there on Nelson and Pa's handiwork. Right there on the flat roof above the porch. Pa's gift. Another man stood beside him in darker clothes. Both white. The first, wearing dark trousers, a white shirt and a tie. A tie. He broke into the door attached to the triangular roof that was not a roof at all once you walked through what looked like windows. It was an entrance to Momma and Pa's room. He disappeared for a few minutes, handed some things to the second guy still on the balcony. He went back in. For a moment, it looked like nothing was happening. Until I saw the tie again. He walked out;

coolly, like him being atop a roof on this side of town was a part of a perfectly normal morning. Then, I saw it. The smoke. The big, cloudy smoke. It found places to ooze out of from the roof top to closed windows. It wrapped around the top of the house in a matter of seconds. The men escaped the fire that had been set by jumping the rail-less balcony. Then, I heard something rumble above like thunder. Reluctantly, I looked away and up through the trees. There were still dark clouds in the sky up there, but it was not from the house burning. The clouds were too straight, too perfect. Aeroplanes. Like the Germans invading France and Belgium. Like I read about in the 'papers. This was happening here. In Tulsa. The Promised Land. Gunshots that were too fast for a pistol went going. Too fast for a finger pulling a trigger. I turned on my stomach and stayed low. The pain in my leg did not matter. The dirt and cold ground under my chin did not matter. I did not feel my tears until my eyes started stinging and kept me from seeing the grass and trees in front of me. Whipping quickly, I looked behind me. Listened. Watched. My heart was beating fast and I wished I had only been spying on nothing more but A.C. or Edith. If only I could turn back time. Could I have stopped this somehow? My warning to the folks in Dreamland was not enough. What was happening to the men who had gone to the courthouse? Pa and Nelson? A.C.? The Army veterans? Mr. Williams? Mr. Ray and the others? What's going to happen to me?

I finally looked down, wincing against the pain that I knew would come. There was a lot of blood. Too much blood. Dark against my skin. My arms went frantic and I started touching anything I could to find something sturdy on the ground. Something I could tie together. Something I could cover the hole with. Something that could stop blood. Something. Anything.

Chapter Twenty-Two
Martial Law

"That's my Father's,"

Adam secured the chandelier on the back of a truck and smiled back at me. His mouth was stiff a little, bulging. He turned toward me and spit outward like he was aiming for me. Tobacco. "Shut that nigger up and get her in line."

I kept my chin high and forced myself not to cry. To ignore the pain in my body. Limping less. Walking straighter. To pretend that I was not ashamed.

When I was found, I was watching them. Two white men. Two white men and Blue Eyes. Blue Eyes had on a misshapen hat, white short-sleeved shirt and trousers that were dirty and rising above his ankles. I could tell his family did not have as much ownership as the other white folks. His feet were bare. Though, he was standing atop of broken materials. Things I could not identify were in pieces. To his left was a pile of belongings that did not belong to either of them. Grinning. They grinned like they were enjoying themselves. Blue Eyes had a handful of something. The man to his right had a rifle, fedora and overalls. Boots. To his far left, looking down at all the stuff—stolen goods—was a sheriff or deputy uniformed. Helping? Helping.

With my hands in the air and limping with most of my weight on my right leg, I winced up at the sun. It watched me through the clouds of smoke. Passed 9:00 AM. Where was Gran'ma Jordan? She was a strong and prideful woman, but too fragile for this. Silently, my heart worried for her. Ached for her. For everyone. We were heading toward the National Guard armory is what I heard them say. Though, something told me not to expect to see everyone there. Police, National Guardsmen, white women and other regular looking white folks. I wanted to walk away, but it was too many. Some had stars, badges. Some did not, but they all acted with the same authority over our destinies. In the distance, I saw other lines of us walking with our hands up. Some of us fully clothed from hats to shoes on our feet. Others embarrassed in their bedclothes. They kept their eyes down, feet moving. Before we were picked up, I heard one of

151

the officers say that we were prisoners. Yet, we were not the ones with the guns. Why weren't the white folks being detained? It had to have been about fifty, eighty of us. I heard them say the Convention Hall was full. Next, something about McNulty Park. Then, finally the National Guard armory after they realized some of us were wounded. As if that was hard to see.

As if my eyes had not seen enough, they swam across the painted skies and desolate land surrounding us. I blinked, heavy and fast. This was Greenwood. This, burning piles of ashes, scratched trees and melted metal was Greenwood. Shattered bits of furniture. Bricks that once were walls, chimneys and massive buildings that provided space for laughter, gossip, eating, love, dancing, viewing, experiencing and living. Both sides of Archer from Boston to Elgin. Mount Zion Baptist Church was nowhere to be seen. No Gurley Hotel. No Stratford Hotel. No hotels at all. Just fires, smoke and debris in the distance. Smoking piles of wreckage. Like a tornado had removed everything. Only, this was no natural disaster. This was done by men, women and children. By people. By people like us. Like God? Had the land been an ocean and Greenwood a ship believed to be unsinkable, this would be the moment of disbelief of its manmade defenselessness to destruction. We, the survivors, were being escorted by gunpoint. Spared to feel guilty for those who had not been so lucky. The shoebox. The baby. The screaming Mother. Another thought occurred to me. How in the world did they burn all of those homes with us there? There had to be thousands. Every home on every block. Greenwood had so many blocks. Blocks I could not walk in an hour's time.

A Negro woman of 92 years, not much for getting out of her comfortable home except for church with her family, lie beside me. She was shot three times by someone or people from the white mobs. The white nurses attended her. I thought about Dr. Andrew and his dog. Where was the most able Negro surgeon in America? Why wasn't he here helping? Was he first tending to the other places they mentioned? McNulty Park? Convention Hall? What about the other Negro doctors and nurses? Chas B. Wickham? I knew, but I did not want to know. I did not want to think so hopelessly. An old man, deaf, dumb and paralytic died of his wounds. My tears were warm, but I knew they could not change much.

"You are wounded. What happened here? Take a look at this, is this a bullet wound," the Red Cross nurse was not directing her questions to me but a partner at her side.

I frantically searched my body for oozing blood and the hole. Somehow, the blood had stopped, but the pain hit me as soon as I looked at it. My leg. My lower back.

"Stay still," she was looking in the wrong place.

"Where—,"I pulled at my dress and for the first time saw the torn cloth seemingly ripped at its side. It was stained, everywhere but especially there. Dark stains that looked like dried dirt.

"Second bullet. No entry. Only grazed your side near your lower back. Praise God,"

The tears were warm again and unwarranted. I felt guilty. Guilty and silly for crying. I watched the mother and children around me. The men, shame in their eyes for not being able to protect whomever were on their minds. I knew them all, but their eyes were like strangers. Like I was seeing them for the first time. Seeing them outside of our comfortable, prosperous city-within-a-city. They were crying out for loved ones who did not make it. Men, women, children, babies. It all flooded my memory. I did not want to believe that it was so. Children dying in their mother's' arms, women shot down in their homes and men killed trying to protect their families. All of them trying to make it to the tracks. The stories, tears and crying swarmed around me. I dozed off in midst of my crying.

When I woke, a white man with a rifle on his shoulder came. I stretched my neck as far as I could. Listened over all of the noise. He had a market basket in his hand. I could not see what was in it, but it was wrapped. Wrapped in an old lace curtain. When I estimated the size, about a foot long in length, I knew instantly what it was.

"I don't know who its people are," the white man told the guy in charge. "What's his name," I whispered. "Major Paul R. Brown, a Tulsa physician and commanding officer of the sanitary detachment. He's here to help restore some order," the nurse's voice sounded assuring, but I had a feeling she did not see the same destruction I saw. "I just found it lying out there in Africa and brought it here," with that, the man left. With his rifle.

Whites could not come without a military pass. We, all Negroes, were provided with a card showing police protection. These cards allowed us to go into the burnt district or Negro quarters. A lot of folks were living outside of the city detained in the refugee and detention camps. They were investigating folks at the city hall. I heard the elders whispering and discussing what they heard. Much later, there was talk of funerals. Soon, we were ordered not to have funerals for the dead. They could not be held in the churches of the city. A lot of the churches were being used for camps for what they called refugees. Whatever that was. An elder who had been in the Great War kept his ears open. He said there was some military policy preventing funerals in city churches because of the feeling still hovering over and within the city. I thought about my folks. This time, I could not stop myself from crying while the Red Cross lady watched.

Clueless.

Chapter Twenty-Three
Timeless

Calm Daze.

"You have an infection from the wound in your leg."

I did not care. It was the kind of pain that lingered until you had to fall asleep to forget about it, but I did not cry. I was quiet most of the time. Like A.C. when he returned back in February. I could not stop thinking about it. I forced myself not to think about it. I could not go five minutes with it crossing my mind. I tried to think about something else. Watching people. Humming, on occasion to drown out the thought of it. What I did.

I was happy to see the folks who had survived and those who were brave enough to stay. Or forced to stay by the National Guard, special deputies and police. Though I was happy to see them, there was something happening to me. I felt hollow. Like my organs were not inside my body. Like my heart and lungs had nothing to do with my breathing. Like my thoughts were not happening in my own head. My mind replayed everything so vividly. I could still hear the screaming. The crying. Gunfire. Planes. My pulse quickened and reminded me that I was not dreaming. This was it. There was no blinking, tossing and turning. Just me and the real world.

Refugees.

They kept trying to get me to talk, 'xcept my mouth wouldn't move. I did not know what to say anymore.

I never knew exactly how Momma and Pa made it to the Fairgrounds the day of the war. When I was transported there, I was grateful to see they were with Gran'ma Jordan. Every other family, big or small, was not that lucky. I lost count of what day it was. Seeing us all together, folks were saying Nelson skipped town. We did not respond to their guesses. They were so sure of themselves anyway. There was no A.C. Freeman. Just vanished. Maybe with Edith Franklin. Trying to forget about what I did, I searched all over for them from my spot on the ground. They were like figments of my imagination. Like Sarah Page and Dick Rowland. Folks had seemed to forget about them altogether.

There was twelve guards at the Fairground Detention Camp. Armed. Fully equipped, it seemed. Like soldiers. I never knew what a refugee was until now. Had no idea how I – a native of Tulsa and American citizen – could be considered a *refugee*. I heard a white woman use that word in reference to us. She was a part of the American Red Cross.

The displaced refugees.

"How are you," she stopped what she was doing and smiled over at Pa. She had since stopped talking to me, because I never responded. Though, I watched her closely. If I did not know any better, I would have believed she was flirting with him. Though, she felt sorry for us and tried to look concerned. Her eyes gave her away. They grew large at the sight of him. Shyly, she ran a finger behind her ear, taking a strand of sandy hair with it. Once she realized that he was still happily married at the subtle reaching out to Momma, answering, "We are resilient people." Resilient? I did not know the meaning of that word yet, but I liked it. She backed off and returned to her job. Her face grew red, but I think Momma and Pa pretended not to notice. The shy lady and others issued green cards that were called American Red Cross Refugee cards. They had to be signed by a white person willing to vouch for us. Pa spoke with some white man when he saw him near the crowds. When the man looked over, I noticed him. It was Mr. Bradley who used to come by Pa's shop once a month or so. Not Adam who had called us uppity. Mr. Bradley was always one of those folks who usually would greet Pa in his store with a huge grin on his face. This time, he looked over at Pa from head-to-toe like Pa was a stranger. His eyebrows came close together and he cleared his throat before speaking, "Do I know you?"

Momma slid her hand in mine and made us make an about-face, leaving Pa and Mr. Bradley alone. I wanted to watch. To listen. I stretched my neck over my shoulder. It was not a long conversation.

I read Mr. Bradley's lips, "It's business," his right eyelid dipped over his eye and his mouth curled up in a smile.

When Pa turned around, I quickly looked away with the expression on his face burning a hole in my heart. I had never seen Pa look so drained. So defeated. I wanted to do something about it. To say something.

I released Momma's hand and ignored the pains in my leg. I tried to walk like there was nothing wrong with me. It was numbing. I could even feel it in my hip. I smiled like everything was perfect. I smiled at Mr. Bradley like I would if we were standing in the Glass House.

"Good morning, Sir," my chest rose and fell as I took a breath between words. "I guess I'm not too young anymore to know something about war,"

He frowned again, looking down at me like he had looked at Pa. His frown softened when he looked down at what was plastered around my leg.

"Faith," Momma grabbed my wrist. "Excuse us," though Momma was pulling me away, I kept my eyes on Mr. Bradley.

"Sir," he cleared his throat. Looked down at the ground and back at Pa. "Is it a voucher that you need?"

The Missing.
"Spinner!"

"Esla?"

I could not run, but I perked up on a hay stack and reached out for him. All the walking I did early in the day made me tired. He came my way. He had a little limp, but was smiling. His hug was long and grateful. I grew self-conscious about my smell. Lowered my head a little, sniffed. I did not smell too much worse than he did. He took a sloppy seat next to me. I smiled over at him.

"What happened to you," he looked down at my wrapped leg.

"I could ask you the same," he appeared fine other than that limp. He was also wearing the same clothes from that night.

"Oh, well, I survived a lil' fire and bullets. Fell on the railroad. Folks stomped all over me after a truck of white folks pulled up. We were on our way to Kansas when we saw the first fire," his chatter was the same. Bouncy and free. Joy still in his eyes. Though we were in the same war, I knew he had not seen what I saw. Or did what I did.

"You know anything about Ellen and Jon? Have you seen them around here?"

His shoulders dipped. He spit to his far right. "They're not here. Thought I would see them here because I saw'em lined up when the white folks had us walking out this way. They split us up into smaller groups. Scared we were gone do something to'em," he laughed a little. "But they the ones who had the guns. Felt like a big ol' fat squirrel in Arkansas." His neck stretched and his voice was lower. "You see all that land out there with nothing on top of it?"

I nodded, reaching for a rock under the hay. There was nothing more I wanted to say. I was afraid I would say too much.

There was a lot of folks who had not been found. I thought about them and Greenwood. Thursday and Sunday nights. The music. The shops. The offices. The people. Nelson's birthday. Mother's Day. Our new house. All gone. All torched.

I was happy Spinner was still next to me. "I bet there is about three thousands of us here," he looked around. Kept on talking. When I did not say anything back, Spinner assured me that he had seen Ellen and John-Jon escorted to another camp. He was trying to comfort me. I felt they were still alive. That was enough for me. Delores was on the Fairgrounds with us somewhere with her family. I tried to wave at her once when I saw her. When I was getting food. I was alone. She just looked at me and kept on walking, catching up with her folks. I guessed maybe she was angry with me for holding her up, coming home so late that night.

It was easier to talk about the missing folk who we knew had enough means to have either gotten away earlier. Though, we kept quiet about all that. I knew. We all knew, but there was this soft spot that kept us from talking about it or asking questions. Momma never mentioned what I did to Pa. If she did, I would never know. They were not treating me any differently. I think. Now that they heard me talk to Mr. Bradley and talking with Spinner, I may not have been worrying them too much by being silent anymore. I wanted to ask what everyone had seen or did to get away, but my manners kept my mouth quiet. After it took three days for Pa to find Gran'ma Jordan and about a week for her to be released from the Convention Hall, she was not saying too much either. All she told Momma was that she had stood her ground and stayed on her porch. They escorted her off forcibly, torching the place. Taking her screaming and hollering to an internment camp. Like I knew it would, her chin remained high even with the sadness in her eyes. She said she had been taking care of Ms. Mabel who was left in the house. She tried to tell them about her being in the house.

"Did they get her out," Momma's voice was low.

"A mob of angry white folk are as bad as the devil himself. No conscience," is all she said. "No one person to hold responsible."

There was a Negro lawyer who stayed. He was fighting for folks like us. Refugees. Mr. Franklin had all these books like I had seen in Pa's sitting room. Shiny on the spine. Looking important. There was a typewriter and a shiny desk under the tent where he was with two other folks. A woman standing behind the typewriter. A man seemingly reading through one of those books to Mr. Franklin's right. They looked busy. Busy and fearless. Watching them with Mr. Franklin made me wonder more about other folks. Edith and A.C. lingered in the front of my mind. Then Nelson a bit longer. I still had not seen either of them. Have not asked about them, but I wanted to.

Questions.
"How are you feeling?"

Hot with a fever, but I played strong. "Just fine."

They kept asking questions. I kept telling them I was alright. Every time. I still had an infection. I made a joke about maybe it being for us having to sleep on haystacks where the fair kept the livestock. Momma did not laugh. Pa looked at me for a second and eventually left to find work.

I finally asked. Resilient people. Pa explained it this way: he placed his hand over Momma's belly. It had since grown over the weeks. She was a slim woman now with a belly that poked out a little. I saw it in private once. In the tent when she was putting on a thin dress that was given to her by the American Red Cross people. Her belly was smooth, but there was stretching skin that scarred a little to the left above her hip. Pa smiled into Ma's eyes. "No matter how huge this big-headed baby decides to get, your Momma's belly will be resilient. It can stand the stretching," Momma rolled her eyes, but she was smiling. He continued. "It can stretch, adjust itself when she needs to sit down to relax," he guided her to the makeshift bed of hay. She put her weight on him as he eased her down to rest. "When this baby decides to come on out," he looked around, smirked. "In this manger, that belly will whip back into shape like it did with the two of you," he was talking like Nelson was still here. Momma kept smiling, but it was weak. She laid her head back. Closed her eyes. Pa rested a hand on her belly. I smiled. Then, it came back to my mind. Everything. The shoebox. I tried to push the screaming from my memory. The crying. The reaching. The running. The gunfire. I tried. I tried.

I refocused. Watched them. Resting close together on top of a haystack. Gran'ma Jordan was already asleep. I wanted to ask, "Why would God let this happen," but I did not want to spoil their moment of peace.

160

Tent Cities.

"Plenty of folks have already left, John. I know you don't want to leave for Louisiana," Momma spoke to Pa's pride. "Or anywhere with my folks, but we are like property here," Momma's voice was strained. She was trying to keep it low. "Like slaves,"

"Sweetheart, relax. I am doing the best I can,"

"This isn't about you, John," she was moving. "This isn't about you."

"This is our only option," he did not sound defeated, but sure.

"Think about our family—,"

"They will not remove us from a place we worked damn hard to build," he did not have to say anymore.

First, it was days. Then weeks in a makeshift tent city and other irregular housing provided by the American Red Cross. We were not allowed to leave. On the first day, we were given food, water and medical attention. Pa scrambled to find Gran'ma Jordan. Someone escorted him. Now, we were being seen and treated as prisoners. White folks got around freely. It were only Negroes in the internment camps. Of course because we no longer had any homes to go to. There is talk going around about us having to get ahold of our own food. Here for weeks and the white folks were not wanting the American Red Cross helping us anymore. No one has come to look at my leg for a while. It was still covered in pain and wrapped.

Luckily, or maybe unfortunately according to Momma's tone, most of the men and women were released after a white person vouched for them to go out for work. Momma said they still were not free. Given that identification card to wear on their clothes. *Like slaves*. Mr. Bradley's guilt-ridden signature allowed for Pa to work.

"Lord, this can't be it. We weren't made for this kind of living," Religion whispered. "Only being released to turn a profit for white folks,"

Jazz whistled. "It's business, Sweetheart."

It was true. We had to pay for our own meals now. From our own pockets even though most of what we had had been stolen or destroyed. It was an insult to injury as Momma described it. Pa was prepared. He had cash in his socks at the bottom of his shoes. He said it was there only for emergencies and that he would work at the tasks available to get spending money. He was gone for most of the day while the sun was up. He was a part of the crew who voluntarily were cleaning up the debris in Greenwood. Children were going, but he would not allow me. He advised the same to Spinner's family. He would come back, sweaty. Tired. Quiet, like A.C. Like me, before Mr. Bradley and running into Spinner. Sometimes, I wanted to ask Pa what he saw there. Eventually, I did not have to. His body carried the weight of whatever it was he saw. One night, Pa sobbed in Momma's arms for the first time. It was the first time I had felt this kind of sorrow from him.

"He lied there," his voiced cracked. He was quiet for a moment. "A bullet wound to his head. Dried blood covering—covering his shirt. Twisted at the waist."

I wanted to ask who Pa was talking about. I prayed it was not Big-Head. Begged, in my mind. In my heart, in spite of what I knew. For anyone to be lying on the ground like that frightened me. It made me think about the guy shot at the courthouse. Left there. Then, I thought about what I did.

"Shhh," Momma comforted him and his sobs went muffled for the night. So did mine.

A standard laborers' wages for cleaning up debris. Pa went out there again and again despite the image he spoke of. When he was gone, Gran'ma

Jordan took on his comforting duties. She was talking again too. Mostly to Momma. She was nicer to Pa, too. Made it a habit to tell him good morning. I think she was finally accepting just how amazing he and Momma were together. I heard them all talking one night about whites complaining that we were being "spoiled" at the fairgrounds by all the attention we were getting from the Red Cross and other charitable organizations. Complaining, as if our entire world as we once had was not destroyed. As if our loss and suffering was not enough. As if our stay on the fairgrounds were imposing on their comfortable homes. Their comfortable neighborhoods. Comfortable communities that had not been torched.

Homeless. Refugees. Homelessness. That is what it meant.

Bastards.

Restless.

I heard once that the ocean was painfully cold during the winter. I wondered if it felt anything like living in the tents. If Greenwood were a ship, the tents were like debris after the shipwreck. In the night, we clung to it for dear life. I clung to as much hay as I could. That did not make me much warmer.

I was sleeping a lot, but not comfortably. Not because I wanted to. Not because I was lazy. It was because I was really tired. Very tired. The lady with Red Cross finally came to see me. Said my infection was not getting any better and that I needed my rest to heal. She gave me medicine. I thought about Dr. Andrew and wondered what he would have done for me had he still been alive. That is who Pa had seen. I heard him talking with Momma again. I had been pretending to be asleep, peering through my flickering eyelashes. "John, who was it?" He whispered low. Sore eyes. "Was it Nelson?" Her question was faint. A tear rolled down Pa's left cheek. I read his lips, "The Negro surgeon."

Thinking about everything made me feel weaker. Sleepier. I listened to the nurse tell me not to fight my sleep. I was not fighting my sleep. I suddenly felt angry. "Have you ever slept outside for weeks?"

She looked at me funny. Searched for an answer. "No. No, not like this." *Like what then*, I wanted to ask, but she left somewhere before I was able to. Somewhere warm, I imagine.

God.
I saw God today.

What I saw was nothing like we talked about in church that I have heard over the years. The witnessing was nothing like the condemnation slipping from tongues wrapped in judgment born of religious elders' doctrines. It was not like the promise folks gave when they told you to shut up with your grieving and just *pray*. It was not like that at all. It was not something I had wished for. Hoped for. Had faith for. Had not prayed for it. But, it happened. It was a subtle mutual acknowledgment. Something I would have ignored had I not known to pay close attention to what I was about to see.

No matter being sick, I was getting better at pretending like I was okay so that I could go with Pa. It took some convincing, but he finally let me. Momma stayed behind to rest.

"Can you keep a secret, Pumpkin Head?"

I looked up at Pa, "Depends on how juicy it is," I laughed, protecting my eyes from the sun with my left hand.

He looked around the desolate Negro District, smiling. At what, I don't know. All I saw when I took a look around was handpicked land that looked like squares of missing houses, businesses, schools and churches. The sky stretched and met with a flattened ground of burnt or missing grass. Bricks had been collected and stacked. Long logs and broken wood was stacked in other piles. The road had dirt with deep line trails in it. I counted about ten tents near where we were. Something sticking out of the ground that looked like a water pump a little in the distance.

164

"There's a fine lawyer who is seeing to it that we get this land back into our hands. Get it back into shape," he was talking fast. He moved about. "This here," pointed a dusty boot to a pile of bricks. "Will be the bricks I add to my new store. A lil' beat up because of the fire, but it gots more meaning to it, now," he laughs. "This here," He picks up the top red brick that looked like it had been melted by lava. The sun danced with Pa. The sky bright and holding God's promise. "This here will be added to our new house I will be building for us. We ain't going nowhere. Won't let the lives we lost be in vain," I thought about Nelson. "We have to leave something here for the folks who will come long after us. This is our legacy. Tulsa's Legacy. Too proud a people to burn us out, ain't that right," he laid down the brick, crouching down with his knees bent and looking over at me with his eyes squinting against the sun. His smile was twisted, but certain. The identification card set on the left side of his chest. He was waiting on me to say something. I did not know what to say, just felt full. Felt full and proud that he was my Pa. That God allowed him to still be here in spite of everything. In spite of what I had done. He pulled the fedora off his head and set it on mine. "What you got in that lil' ol' round head of yours,"

I did not say anything to him, just fell in his lap and hugged his neck. He fell back losing his footing and laughed. He smelt like outside and sweat, but it did not bother me.

When we were back on our feet and wiping the dirt and dust off our clothes, I noticed someone walking by. Working, I think. It was not a man.

Standing to my feet after having fallen to the ground with Pa made me remember that I was faking being alright. When I twisted and lifted my body to watch her, Pain pierced my leg and made its way up to my hip. I winced, but pretended it never happened. Pa was talking, but I could not hear him. "Give me a second, Pa,"

"Where are you going?"

"Just to ask a quick question!"

"Esla,"

"Just a second, Pa!"

Something was happening to me, but I did not care. I tried my best to make my way to her. "Excuse me! Hey! Excuse me," my voice sounded hoarse in my ear. She paused. Searched. I came to a stop, out of breath. "Where is A.C.," the question fell out of my mouth without any courtesy.

"It is good to see you," She smiled. "I have been watching you,"

"Me," I was confused.

She nodded. "He told me about Greenwood's young explorer—you," she was still smiling. "We were accident waiting to happen. A.C. and I."

I blinked, but it was heavy. Uncontrolled. I tried to open my eyelids. Keep them open. Looked at her. She pulled the oversized fedora from her head. The wind danced with her hair. I was dizzy. Blinking. Blind.

Momma would say that I have learned my lesson for being so nosy. While grieving, of course. Pa would say I have gotten my wish to being unforgettable. Except, I probably would not make it into the Tulsa Star newspaper. Or any newspaper for that matter. Tulsa Star was gone. Everything was gone. The Tulsa Tribune, still standing in the white district, was certainly not reporting anything about little Black girls dying in the middle of Little Africa. No college. No Howard or Harvard. No reports of being a graduate. No cheesy, proud picture of me in the graduates' column. Ellen and John-Jon would be proud. Proud that I put away the trouble in spying and just went on up and asked for what I wanted to know. They could tell Spinner about the time Ellen fell off the taxi. Or when we went spying on folks. Or when we used to beat up the Carlton kids so long ago. Aunt Angela was right. A.C. would tell me to be sure to ask God as many questions as I could think of.

The first question I am going to ask does not take much thinking at all. I would be sure God could hear every word. Though, it would probably be known before I could say them. It was important for me to ask. To receive an answer. For me to know, for the short time I had.

"What was my purpose?"

Made in the USA
San Bernardino, CA
01 July 2018